Byte
The Computer Mite

Text copyright©2012 Alec Rowley
Cover design©Felix Leone
Illustrations©Felix Leone
All rights reserved
ISBN 978-0-9566342-2-1
First Edition

SURREY LIBRARIES	
Askews & Holts	01-May-2012
JF	£6.99

Hawkwood Books 2012

For
Betsy and Newman

The Bits of This Story

Bit 0: Midnight Meetings

Byte was the busiest creature on The Inside. Millions of messages a second, endless instructions, do this, do that. But who was on The Outside telling him what to do? This was one of The Big Questions and he had to find the answer.

He lay down his bundle of atoms and stretched, looked up and caught a glimpse of Outside Light. He stretched and grew, raced upwards, bounced on a wire and landed on a small, ivory ledge.

Peotry Willow heard the faint thump even in her sleep and woke to the sound. She turned to see a figure swaying on a single key of her computer keyboard, a tiny creature with eyes that were pinpricks of pure brilliance.

"Hello," said Peotry.

"Hello," said Byte.

"Who are you?" asked Peotry.

"You can call me Byte," said Byte. "Who are you?"

"You can call me Peotry," said Peotry, "because that's my name."

Which was all it took to make firm friends.

"What are you doing here?" asked Peotry.

"I have come to see The Outside," said Byte. "Will you show me?"

"I can show you bits of it," said Peotry, "but I'm only six. My brother and sister can show you more than me."

Byte had no idea what brothers and sisters were. He realised there were basics to learn before The Big Questions could be asked.

Peotry said, "I've got two brothers and one sister," and tried to explain what they were. "How many do you have?" she asked.

Byte pondered a moment. He thought he understood a little.

"About fifty million," he said, "give or take a few."

"That's an awful lot," said Peotry. "Do you know their names?"

Byte shook his head.

"I suppose not," said Peotry. "Won't they miss you?"

"They'll want me back," said Byte, "to work. But they won't miss me."

"That's sad," said Peotry. "If I was gone, my family would miss me."

"Well there aren't many of you," said Byte. He considered this a moment, then said, "Couldn't they get another you?"

"Another me? Oh, no. You are silly. I'm the only one of me. I'd be gone forever and they'd be sad."

Byte felt obliged to explain that there were many things about The Outside that he didn't know, and 'sad' was one of them.

"I'll have to teach you everything," said Peotry.

"That would be excellent," said Byte. "That's why I came out, Peotry, to learn. For instance, what's this thing I'm sitting on?"

"I thought you lived in it," said Peotry.

"I do," said Byte, "but I don't know what it is."

"Well, that's a keyboard. You press the keys and it makes things happen on my computer."

"I'm pressing it," said Byte. "I'm sitting on it, but nothing's happening."

"That's because you have to turn on the electricity first, then it goes."

"Show me," said Byte.

Peotry switched on her computer. The screen flickered into life.

"Ah, I see!" Byte whispered to himself, and then to Peotry, "The Power!"

Peotry looked blank. This strange little creature was either very clever or very silly, but he didn't seem dangerous. Although Peotry had been taught never to talk to strangers, she didn't think it mattered if the stranger was only half an inch tall.

"The Power," said Byte, "gives us life and instructs us. The Power turns the darkness to light."

Byte jumped onto the table. He stared at the computer, not particularly impressed.

"So that's what it looks like," he said. "I always wondered. Show me what it does, Peotry."

"Watch," said Peotry.

She started playing a fast-moving game in which a funny little figure raced to dodge endless nasty traps.

"When does it start?" Byte asked.

"It's started," said Peotry, "but I never get much further than this."

"That's because you're too slow," said Byte. "Shall I help you?"

"You're too small," said Peotry. "You couldn't press the keys."

"Keys are no good," said Byte. "You have to join in. Watch!"

Byte walked around the back of the computer, jumped into the ventilation slot and disappeared. Peotry expected a puff of smoke and an explosion because she knew it was dangerous to tamper with electricity.

But nothing happened.

Until.

Suddenly.

The figures on the screen began to move. They speeded up and threw themselves around faster and faster and faster until all Peotry saw were streaks of light on the monitor. She clapped her hands in delight.

Then up came the message,

Level 1 Completed.
2500 points.

Press any key to start Level 2

Byte jumped out.

"Was that alright?" he asked.

"Alright?" Peotry laughed. "Not even Ryan is as fast as that. How did you do it?"

"How did you **not** do it?" asked Byte. "It's very easy, just a beginning and an end. Is this what you call a game?"

"Yes. I've lots more. And we've got them at school as well."

"What's school?" asked Byte.

"School's where we go to learn," said Peotry.

Byte gave this a few moments consideration, staring at the ceiling as if hoping to see a school emerge out of nothing. He looked around the room which he thought was the entire Outside, searching in vain for a school.

"You'll have to show me this 'school'," he said. "I need to learn. I need to know The Outside and answer The Big Questions. Where are your brothers and your sister?" Byte asked.

"That's not a Big Question," said Peotry. "They're asleep in their rooms. It's late."

"Their rooms?" Byte asked, puzzled. "Is there more than one Outside?"

"This isn't the whole Outside," said Peotry. "It's my bedroom. The Outside is much bigger than this. It's a whole world."

"Oh!" exclaimed Byte. "Is it twice as big?"

"No. Much bigger."

"Ten times?"

"Bigger still. Millions of times bigger."

Byte sat down on the mouse mat.

"This is only a bedroom," said Peotry. "We've got four bedrooms in this house and there are lots of houses in the block and lots of blocks in the city and..."

"Stop!" ordered Byte. "Let me go one atom at a time. I see I shall have to keep an open mind. I hope it's open enough to take in all there is to learn. Now tell me, what's this?"

"This is a lamp," said Peotry. "You can make the room light in the dark."

Peotry pressed the switch.

"Is it too bright?" she asked.

"Is it on yet?" Byte replied.

"Of course it's on!" Peotry said.

"So it is," Byte said, squinting. "It's a dark kind of light, isn't it? When things are on the move in there," he said, pointing to the computer, "it's like thousands of these. Millions."

That sounded like a whole lot of light.

"Doesn't it hurt your eyes?"

"You get used to it," Byte replied.

"My teacher says if you look directly at the sun you can go blind."

"What's a sun?" Byte asked.

"It isn't 'a' sun," Peotry said, "it's *The* Sun. There's only one and it's brighter than a million billion lamps all on at the same time."

"Can I see it?" asked Byte.

"Not now. It's night time. You can see it in the morning."

"Ah," moaned Byte, "night time and morning, suns and schools. Worlds within worlds. So many words to learn! But I will go one atom at a time. What's this?"

"It's a flower. A daffodil. I'm growing it for my school competition."

Byte ignored all the words he did not understand and concentrated on what he wanted to know and to see.

"Lift me up," he said. "I would like to see the yellow blob at the top."

"Alright," said Peotry. "Stand on my hand."

Byte stood on Peotry's hand and cried "Ooh!" as she lifted him up and he fell on his backside.

"Slowly! Slowly!"

Peotry lifted him higher until he was level with the petals. Regaining his balance, Byte stood open-mouthed.

"Do you like it?" asked Peotry.

Byte leaned over to touch it and Peotry held him close to the petal. He squeezed it gently between his fingers and felt the soft texture of the leaf.

"Higher," he said.

Peotry lifted him up and Byte jumped out onto the golden flower. He walked up and down, touched the inside of the petals, put his tiny nose to their silky sides, sniffed and smiled, then sat down in the central hollow which was perfectly shaped for his little body.

"Do you like it?" Peotry asked again. There was no answer so Peotry peered closer. Byte was engrossed, exploring the inside of the daffodil.

"I have not been in this world long," he said, "and there are so many mysteries, but the most mysterious of all is this yellow softness. It is so gentle and it says 'Hello' to me. I shall stay here while I am with you, Peotry. This will be my new home."

Peotry was delighted. He looked very comfy, but Peotry had a sudden worrying thought.

"It doesn't live long," she said. "Soon it will die and your home will fall down. What will you do then, Byte?"

Byte considered. He didn't fully understand life and death on The Inside let alone The Outside.

"I think it will live long enough for me," he said, finally. "What did you call it?"

"A daffodil."

Byte stared at Peotry, fascinated.

"Do you know that I am smaller than the blue in the middle of your eyes?" he asked. "And you are bigger than anything I ever imagined."

"Why did you leave?" Peotry asked. "Weren't you happy?"

As she spoke, her breath made the flower sway backwards and forwards and Byte had to hold on not to tumble out.

"I left because I was too busy," he said. "I have to work fast and hard. Fetch and carry, carry and fetch, do this, do that, and what for? I want to find out why I work so hard. I want to meet The Power. Do you know everything there is to know, Peotry?"

"I'm only six," Peotry replied. "I can read and write and do a few sums, but I don't know everything."

"What about this place you called school? Do people know everything there?"

"The teachers do," said Peotry, "though I don't think they would know about you."

"What happens at school?" asked Byte.

"We read books," said Peotry. "We do things. We find out how everything works."

"Then it is your teacher I have to meet," said Byte. "I have to see everything. Why is this flower yellow, Peotry, can you tell me?"

"I can't," she answered, "but if you were bigger you could look in a book."

"Show me a book."

Peotry went to the bookcase and brought out a few a few of her favourites. She showed one to Byte. It was the story of 'Jack and the Beanstalk'. He squinted, trying to figure out how it worked.

"What's in it?" he asked.

"You don't know anything, do you, Byte?"

"I can't help it, Peotry. I have come to learn, so you can be my teacher. What's a story?"

"A story is something which isn't true."

Byte considered this, but without much understanding.

"If it isn't true, why talk about it?" he asked. "Isn't your world within worlds full enough without making things up?"

"I'll tell you what," said Peotry. "I'll read you 'Jack and the Beanstalk' and then you might understand what a story is."

"Good idea," said Byte. "What do I have to do?"

"You don't have to do anything. You just sit there in the daffodil and listen."

So Byte sat back in the flower and listened while Peotry read. When she had finished there was silence for a moment, then a sudden knock on the door and Peotry's father came in.

"Peotry!" he said. "What are you doing up? It's midnight!"

"I was reading 'Jack and the Beanstalk' to Byte, Daddy. He came out of the computer and wants to learn about the world. He's sitting inside the daffodil."

"I see," said Mr Willow. "Right. Now you climb back into bed and go to sleep. Go on."

Peotry did as she was told, but as soon as her father had gone, she got out of her bed again and peeked into the daffodil.

"Are you still there Byte?" she whispered.

"Was that the giant?" Byte replied.

"That was my dad."

"He is big," said Byte. "He scared me. Peotry?"

"Yes?"

"Do you think I've done the right thing?"

"What do you mean?"

"Coming into your world. This is a very unsafe place. A little thing like me could get squished."

Peotry didn't want to lose Byte. He was already her special friend and she would be desperate if he decided to return home so soon. As for the idea of him getting squished, that was unthinkable.

"You mustn't go back," she pleaded. "I'll look after you. I can show you to my friends. They'll love you."

"I don't want to be shown to anyone," Byte objected. "You must keep me a secret. Now read me another story."

"Alright," said Peotry, "then I'll have to go to bed. But first, I have to teach you a word?"

"Of course."

"It's 'please'. If you ask anyone to do something for you, you must say 'please'."

"Why is that?"

"You just do. It's good manners."

"Well, alright. I don't understand, but I will say 'please'. I am so used to having to do things. You see there are laws where I come from, and if the law says 'Do This', it must be done, and if the law says 'Do That', it must be done. The laws don't say 'please'."

"I'll read you Cinderella," said Peotry.

"Please," said Byte.

A little way into the story, the bedroom door opened and Mrs Willow came in.

"Peotry! Daddy told you just now to go to sleep."

"But I'm reading to Byte. He's in the daffodil."

"Then Byte will have to wait until morning. You must go to sleep. Go on, into bed."

Again Peotry did as she was told, but this time, when her mother was gone she stayed in bed.

"Are you still there, Byte?"

"Yes I am. Was that Cinderella?"

"No. That was my mum. And she was angry."

"Why?"

"Because I'm being naughty."

Byte didn't know what 'naughty' meant but he didn't care; he was thinking about the story.

"Please read me the end of Cinderella, Peotry, please, please, please!"

"I can't," Peotry answered. "I have to go to sleep now."

"I said 'please'. I said it many times."

"That doesn't matter. You can't always get what you ask for, even if you say 'please'."

Byte was puzzled. He had carried out Peotry's instructions exactly and yet what happened wasn't what was supposed to happen.

"Aren't there any laws here?" he asked. "What's the point of saying 'please' if the thing you're asking for still doesn't get done?"

A possibility dawned on him. On The Inside the law said, 'If you are told, do it', but very often things couldn't be done. They simply *couldn't* be done. The mystery was why the law told them to do something that couldn't be done. Perhaps, thought Byte, there were two types of laws. One type came from people like Peotry and her parents, and it was quite clear these laws were bendable. Another type was the un-bendable law of The Power which Byte and all his kind followed. The law which didn't say 'please'. When the laws bumped into each other...

Byte stood up, suddenly alert. Millions of times he had been stumped inside his speeding world, told to go to a place that did not exist, not knowing what to do. This was impossible, and yet it happened. The Power could not be wrong, there was no wrongness in his world, but something made things go wrong and now he knew what - Human Errors! Like Peotry and her mother and her father. They gave instructions that could not be followed, that could lead to all kinds of confusions. If he learned nothing else, this was worth knowing. Human Errors!

"Thank you, Peotry," he called out, but there was no answer. "Thank you, Peotry."

Byte looked out of the bell of the daffodil. Peotry lay in her bed and her eyes were closed.

"What a strange thing to do," Byte said. "I hope she has not died already. I will do the same thing as her. Let me see... lay down... eyes closed... ah, yes. I understand..."

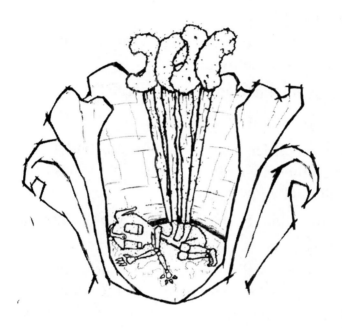

Let me see... lay down... eyes closed... ah, yes. I understand...

Bit 1: Breakfast

"Beth!"

"Go away!"

"Beth! Wake up! It's me, Peotry! I have to show you something!"

"Go away, Peotry. I'm still asleep."

"No you're not. You're awake."

Peotry's older sister snuggled up under the bedclothes, but no amount of snuggling could make Peotry give up.

"Come on, Beth, get up. We've got a visitor."

"Don't be silly, Peotry. It's early in the morning. It's very early in the morning. You've been dreaming, now go back to sleep."

"No, I haven't, it's real. He's real. He came in the night, Beth, honestly."

Beth thought vaguely that perhaps a relative might have turned up unexpectedly; unusual but possible.

"Who is it?" she mumbled from under the bedclothes. "Uncle Joe? Aunt Irene? Father Christmas?"

"It's Byte!"

"Never heard of him."

"Of course you haven't, Beth. He's new."

Beth was forced to open her eyes and turn to her excited little sister. Peotry's eyes were bright with expectation.

"What are you on about, Peotry?"

"I'm on about Byte, Beth. He's come out of the computer."

"Peotry?"

"Yes?"

"Go away," and Beth pulled the covers over her head and closed her eyes. Peotry sighed and left Beth alone to whatever thoughts and dreams kept her so soundly tucked up in bed. She went into the next bedroom.

"Ryan?"

"Mmm?"

"Get up, Ryan, quickly! Come and see Byte."

Ryan mumbled something rude, his hearing almost blocked out completely by the earpieces of an iPod and a soft down pillow. Peotry lifted the left earpiece and whispered into her brother's ear, "It's something to do with computers."

Still Ryan didn't budge. His long, lanky body just shifted slightly in bed.

"He's tiny," insisted Peotry. "He lives in the computer and can make games go superduperfast. You can win anything."

Ryan opened an eye then closed it again. Who'd have a baby sister!

He clamped the pillow around his ears and carried on thinking about Trisha of the Upper Sixth.

Peotry thought William, at eight months old, was too young to persuade and went into her parents' bedroom instead.

"Up already?" her father asked.

"Byte thought you were the giant from 'Jack and the Beanstalk', and he thought mum was Cinderella."

"Did he?" asked Mrs Willow. "Why did he think that?"

"I was reading him the story when you came in."

"Oh, yes, I remember. Who gave you the idea about Byte, Peotry? It's very sweet."

"It's not an idea, Mum, it's real. He popped up through the computer keyboard to see the world. He says he has to work all the time. Do this. Do that. That's why he left."

"Very sensible, too," said Mr Willow, joining in the joke. "Wish I could do the same."

Peotry's parents, were, as parents went, pretty good. They loved her, they loved all their four children and they had a happy enough home, but they were too doubting to believe in silly stories.

"Byte said he wondered what it was all about."

"Even more sensible!" said Mr Willow. "If he finds out, will you ask him to tell me, Peotry?"

Peotry felt her father and mother didn't believe her at all.

"We do believe you, Peotry," Mrs Willow said. "He sounds like a very wise little, erm..."

"Mite," Mr Willow suggested, about to burst out laughing. "Something small. Like a speck of dust. A mite."

"Yes," said Mrs Willow. "He sounds like a very wise little mite."

Peotry knew that her parents weren't serious so she stamped her foot and hurried into William's bedroom. William was in his cot, awake, playing with some of his toys.

"William," said Peotry. "You must promise that when you grow up you won't be like *them*!" she said, turning up her nose. "Aren't they all so stupid! Well, they must find out. If they don't, Byte might get thrown away by mistake, or hurt."

William gurgled his approval to everything his sister said.

"I hate it when they don't believe me," said Peotry. "You probably don't either, but you're too small to say so. What shall I do? Now, let me see…"

The Willows liked to eat together and at eight o'clock they gathered together at the breakfast table.

Ryan and Beth both looked like they'd been dragged backwards through a hedge and only slightly more awake than when Peotry had left them. Beth's thick black hair was a wild tangle of knots.

"Your hair looks like it hasn't been combed for months," said Mrs Willow.

"I'll do it after breakfast," muttered Beth.

"And you," said Mrs Willow to Ryan, "look indescribably horrible."

Ryan smoothed out his hair.

"Where's Peotry?" he asked. "She was in my bedroom trying to wake me up with some silly story."

"And mine," said Beth. "Perhaps she's sulking."

"She was awake at midnight, poor thing," said Mr Willow. "Said she was reading 'Jack and the Beanstalk' to a little creature that had popped out of her computer."

They all laughed.

"Well at least she's telling us the same story," said Ryan. "That's what she told me, too."

"And me," said Beth.

"And me," said Mrs Willow. "Except it was 'Cinderella'."

They looked at each other and there was a moment of quiet.

"Perhaps we're not giving her enough time," said Mr Willow. "She's trying to get our attention. Peotry!" Mrs Willow called out. "Peotry! Breakfast!"

"You should have called her 'Poetry'," said Ryan. "She's always imagining things."

"It was the nearest we could think of," said Mrs Willow. "Peotry is a beautiful name."

"I like it," said Peotry, coming in and taking her place at the table, very calmly.

"You won't when you grow up," said Ryan. "You'll wish they'd called you Jane or Susan."

"What have you got in your hands, Peotry?" her mother asked.

"It's Byte," said Ryan, smirking. "She's giving him a cuddle."

Beth laughed and Mr Willow smiled. Mrs Willow also found it difficult not to laugh.

So Peotry took what she was holding from beneath the table and carefully laid it down in the centre of the breakfast table, covered by a handkerchief. Then, like a well-practised magician she drew away the handkerchief.

Absolute silence. No laughter. No smiles. Not a sound. Just wonder and amazement, all rolled into one.

Byte sat in an open matchbox that Peotry had lined with a tiny piece of cotton wool.

"Peotry!" cried Beth.

"I don't believe it!" whispered Ryan.

"Good Lord!" whispered Mr Willow.

Mrs Willow just stared.

Byte stared back, standing up on the soft fluffy cotton wool, turning around, looking at them, one after the other.

"Hello," he said. "I'm Byte."

Nobody answered.

"They're shocked," said Peotry, "not rude. I told you Byte, they didn't believe me. Mummy, this is Byte."

"Hello, Byte." Mrs Willow's voice was thin and faint.

"Daddy, this is Byte."

Mr Willow nodded.

"Byte, this is Ryan and this is Beth."

"Hello, Ryan. Hello, Beth."

"Peotry!" Beth exclaimed again. "It's true!"

"Of course it's true. I don't tell lies, Beth."

"But it's not possible," whispered Mr Willow. "This kind of thing doesn't happen."

"Apparently it does," said Mrs Willow. "Peotry, he's so... so..."

"Small, Mum, yes, I know. He has to be or he couldn't live inside my computer."

"In your computer!" said Mr Willow. "Come on, Peotry, computers don't work with little men running around inside them."

"I am not a little man," said Byte. "I am Byte."

"He talks so funny," said Beth.

"I shall wake up in a moment," said Mr Willow, "and this will all be a silly dream. Look. I'm closing my eyes and telling myself to wake up. After three. One. Two. Three....Oh..."

Byte was looking questioningly into Mr Willow's open eyes.

"It's not a dream," said Peotry. "He's real."

They all started talking at the same time, asking questions, staring, pointing, laughing, as if they were all children again and Peotry was the adult showing them something new and wonderful. Where... How... When... Why... and so on. Peotry couldn't answer the barrage of questions until they calmed down.

"Where does he really come from, Peotry?" asked Ryan. "I mean really?"

"I told you. He popped out of my computer. Byte, you tell them."

"It's true," said Byte.

"Prove it," said Ryan.

"He did prove it," said Peotry. "To me."

"How?"

"In his own way. Now, I think," said Peotry, enjoying this sudden celebrity, "that it's rude to talk about him as if he's not here. Ask him."

Ryan looked at Byte and felt rather awkward.

"I can't," he said. "I mean, I feel silly talking to such a little...erm..." Byte looked offended. "I... I..." stuttered Ryan.

"You're useless," said Peotry. "Daddy, you talk to him."

"I'm afraid I... I..."

"Oh Dad, you're just as bad."

Then Beth said, "Hello Byte."

"Hello Beth."

"Do you really live inside Peotry's computer?"

Byte nodded. Beth clapped her hands.

"He's lovely!" she cried. "He's gorgeous! Can I look after him, Peotry?"

"No," Peotry answered firmly, still angry that no one had believed her. "You can help me, maybe, but I'm in charge. Are you alright, Byte?"

"I feel quite alright," said Byte. "This is so interesting. I don't mean to upset your family, though, Peotry. Perhaps I should go back?"

"No!" said Peotry, and then Mrs Willow said,

"No, please. I'm sorry, Byte. You see, it's so unusual. And, well..."

"Tell you what," said Ryan, still unable to talk directly to Byte, "if he lives in a computer..."

"My computer," interrupted Peotry.

"Doesn't matter," said Ryan. "They're all the same, almost. Well, he should know his way around a Gamestar, right?"

Gamestars were the biggest selling consoles of the year.

"Why should he?" Beth asked. "You wouldn't know your way around if you were suddenly dropped into a new house, would you?"

Beth had taken sides immediately. She had fallen in love with Byte and thought Ryan was being stupid not to believe Peotry and Byte entirely.

"I'd learn quickly," said Ryan. "Peotry, ask him."

"You ask him."

"I can't."

"Why not?"

"Well, because I can't. He's too small."

"Don't ask, don't get," said Peotry.

"I'll ask," said Beth. "Byte? Do you know what a Gamestar is?"

Byte shook his head.

"Told you," said Ryan. "He doesn't live in a computer at all. He's a fake. Everyone on Earth has heard of a Gamestar."

"Show me," said Byte.

Peotry ordered her brother to fetch his Gamestar in the kind of tone he didn't dare refuse. Ryan shuffled off mumbling something under his breath while Mrs Willow, watching Byte with great fascination, said,

"Do you eat, Byte?"

Byte raised his palms up and out as if to say, 'I don't understand'.

"Food. Eat. Hungry."

"He's not an idiot, Mum," said Peotry.

"I'm sorry," said Mrs Willow. "I just wondered..."

"This is food," said Beth, holding a slice of bread and jam. "Watch!" and she bit a piece from it, chewed it, and swallowed. "Gone!" she said, and showed Byte a piece missing from the bread and jam.

"That is wonderful," said Byte, admiringly. "I have no idea how you did it."

"You mean you don't eat?" asked Mrs Willow. "How do you live, then?"

"I just live," said Byte. "And I have come out of my world to find out how and why. I need to answer The Big Questions."

"If you do," said Mr Willow, "you'll be the first."

"I will? Hmm. I have so many questions to ask. Peotry told me," observed Byte, "that her teacher at school answers all her questions. She can take me to school and I will speak to this teacher."

Mr Willow raised his eyebrows, but he tried not to look too boringly strict.

Ryan came back into the room with his Gamestar. He laid it on the table next to Byte.

"What is it?" asked Byte.

"What is it!" exclaimed Ryan. "And you tell me that he lives in a computer!"

"That's *why* he doesn't know," Beth said. "He doesn't know what they're like from The Outside, only from The Inside."

"Rubbish," said Ryan.

Byte walked around the Gamestar, peeking inside wherever he could.

"I can work it," said Byte, "but you must give me something in return."

"What?" asked Ryan, doubtfully.

"I want to be a secret," said Byte. "I do not like being stared at."

"I can understand that," said Mr Willow. "He's so small, poor chap, it must be very scary."

"Alright," said Ryan. "It's a deal."

Byte began to wonder about these strange, large creatures. The only one he really felt comfortable with, so far, was the one called

Peotry. There was something simple and straightforward about her that he liked.

Ryan switched on the Gamestar. When Byte saw more evidence of The Power he opened his eyes and his mind to learn, but as he listened to Ryan's explanation of the game his little face dropped and he looked pitifully at Ryan. Ryan misunderstood the look.

"Too hard?" Ryan asked.

"I don't think so," Byte said.

"It's taken me weeks just to get to Level 3," said Ryan. "It's a killer." Byte raised his tiny eyebrows in puzzlement. "It's unbeatable," Ryan explained.

"But there is nothing to beat," said Byte, puzzled. "There is a beginning and an end and that is all. You are just too slow to see it."

"Too slow!" Ryan exclaimed. "Hah!" Ryan was a whiz at computer games. He had never been called slow before in his life.

Byte asked Peotry to lift him onto the Gamestar. He walked around a little, then, in an instant, was gone.

"Where did he go?" Beth asked, worried.

"He's gone to join in," said Peotry. "Watch."

"I hope he doesn't get electrocuted," said Mrs Willow.

"Ssh!" said Peotry. "It's beginning."

They all leaned over the table and watched the screen. Ryan had reset the game to Level One.

"What happens," he said to everyone, "is that the hero has to get through all the levels. In each level there are monsters and traps and you only have three lives. If you do the wrong thing, you're dead. Kaput. In the magazines it says that no one has ever got passed Level Nine. There's a rumour that Level Ten doesn't exist, that..."

Ryan's voice trailed off as he watched the hero nimbly bypass the obstacles of Level One and into Level Two.

Ryan opened and closed his mouth, but nothing came out. Peotry stuck her tongue out at him. Beth smiled a great big smile. Mrs Willow looked puzzled and Mr Willow fascinated.

Level Three. Level Four. Level Five.

The hero was dodging around as easily as could be. The monsters and demons got nowhere near him.

Level Six. Level Seven.

Ryan stared. He thought the game would end any moment, but it didn't. It even speeded up and the monsters and demons flared and vanished.

Level Eight. Level Nine. Level Ten.

The screen suddenly came to a halt and the message appeared,

You Win!

The Quest is Ended!

There were various scores which were all, in a word, perfect.

And out popped Byte.

Ryan stared at the little creature in astonishment.

"That was brilliant," he said. "Brilliant! Wait till...", but Mr Willow's warning finger stopped him.

"A deal is a deal," Mr Willow said.

"Was it successful?" Byte asked.

"Successful!" Ryan exclaimed. "You got to Level 10. You did it! I didn't even believe there *was* a Level Ten!"

"There is only a beginning and an end," said Byte. "Already I have learned why the law cannot always be obeyed. This is because there are two laws, one from The Power and one from Human Errors. And now I have learned how we look into each other's worlds but see only our own. This is all a puzzle, but a good beginning. When I return I shall be most wise."

"But you're not going to return," Peotry asked, "are you, Byte?"

"I would like to stay outside for as long as I can," said Byte. "But I will go back one day. I have to."

Peotry hoped it wouldn't be for a long time.

"You'll have to be very careful," said Mrs Willow. "You're a tad small and this is a big, fast world."

"Things are big," said Byte, "but they are not fast."

"I'll look after him, Mum," said Peotry. "He'll be fine."

Mr Willow stared at Byte and shook his head. Part of him still refused to believe this was not a dream.

"He's brilliant," repeated Ryan. "He's a genius! Just think what he could do!"

Byte looked concerned at Ryan's enthusiasm. This medium sized Human Error seemed the most wild of all and the most dangerous.

"Don't worry, Byte," said Peotry. "Ryan's alright. He'll keep his promise."

Ryan's face dropped a little.

"Only if Byte wants me to," he said. "He can always change his mind and let me take him to school. Our technology teacher will have a fit. After all the things she's taught us, to find out a little man lives inside our computer? That's hysterical!"

"You mustn't tell" said Beth. "You promised. We all did. I did too."

"I know, I know," said Ryan.

"Byte," asked Mr Willow, hesitantly. "Do you know about big computers as well as small ones?" Byte looked questioningly at Mr Willow. "I was just wondering..."

"Daddy!" said Peotry. "Are you going to ask Byte to do something for you at work? You shouldn't, you know."

"It's alright, Peotry," said Mr Willow. "I was just thinking aloud. You see, Byte, I use computers a lot in my job..."

"Job?" Byte asked.

"Yes, my job. What I have to do every day to earn money. You know what money is?"

Byte shook his head.

"Well, that doesn't matter. The thing is, we have a very difficult problem at work at the moment, and it seems to me you might be able to help. If you wanted to, that is. And no one need know about you. Just an idea. You don't have to say yes or no now. Think about it a little."

"I would like to help," said Byte, "if I can."

"You can help me," said Beth. "I bet you could! We've got computers in our class at school. I could really show off to the others and do some amazing things!"

"Beth!" Peotry exclaimed, exasperated at her family who a few minutes ago didn't believe in Byte but were now asking him to do them all favours.

"You don't have to," said Beth, "but if you help Dad and Ryan, you could help me, too. It would be very easy and I wouldn't have to tell anyone about you."

"You would," said Peotry. "You'd tell everyone. No one will keep Byte a secret except me."

"And me," said Mrs Willow. "Though I was just thinking..."

"Mummy!" cried Peotry. "Don't listen to them, Byte. If you do you'll be with them all the time and never with me and I'm the one you came to see, not them, and you won't learn anything and you'll be working harder than ever."

"I shouldn't like that," Byte said. "I have never been asked so much and told so little. It's usually the other way around, you see. I think it will take me time to learn how to choose."

Mrs Willow sighed and said, "Time's pressing, everyone. You three have to get to school, we have to get to work and none of us are ready. Peotry, are you going to take Byte with you?"

Of course she was going to take Byte to school! This was what Byte himself wanted to do. He hadn't come into the world to be a stay-at-home. The family watched, fascinated, as Byte walked on to Peotry's hand and Peotry disappeared into her bedroom.

They each looked at the other, fit to burst.

"This is great," said Ryan, breaking the silence, "just great!"

In her room, Peotry looked at her new friend and said, "How should I carry you, Byte? You'll need a safe place to hide in."

She looked around and saw her toy calculator.

"Hmm," said Byte. "It will do," and without another word he disappeared inside it.

"Byte," Peotry called. "Are you there?"

On the screen, she read, "I'm here."

Now Peotry had something no other child on the whole planet had.

She had Byte.

And she had something every other child on the planet had.

She had school.

Ryan and Beth both looked like they'd been dragged backwards through a hedge

Bit 2: Byte Goes To School

Mr Wallis always had at least half a dozen things going on in the classroom at any one time and usually was not in control of any of them.

He was a tall and bulky man, a real giant to the six year old children in his class and was forever knocking himself on the tables and chairs, though he somehow managed to avoid the children. He shouted a lot, but no one took any notice of the shouts, even the angry ones. In fact it was a game to see how quickly you could make him lose his temper.

This wasn't a difficult game to win.

He was always very busy, too busy to stop and answer questions. "Just a minute," he would say, and then he'd forget all about you.

It was a miracle any work got done at all, especially art and craft. The paints were so messy it was impossible to tell one colour from another. A junk box in the corner had overturned so there were plastic bottles, egg boxes, cardboard tubes and the like all over the place.

However, despite all this, the children liked him as they would a big, cuddly teddy bear.

Every morning the class had a 'Show and Tell' lesson after register where Mr Wallis would listen to some of the children tell the class about things they had brought to school. Peotry arrived that morning a little late, just as 'Show and Tell' was about to start. Beth waited at the door, half hoping Byte would jump out the calculator and make himself known to the class, but he didn't, so Beth went off, reluctantly, to her own class.

"Peotry, you're late," said Mr Wallis. "That's not like you. Come and sit down. Jennifer is about to tell us what she's brought. Go on Jennifer."

Jennifer Bradshaw stood up but remained mysteriously silent.

"What's the matter, Jennifer?"

Jennifer shook her head from side to side.

"Don't you want to Show and Tell?"

Jennifer kept shaking her head.

"Alright, sit down," and Jennifer sat down, nothing to show, nothing to tell.

"Who's next?" asked Mr Wallis, fearing a disastrous lack of showing and telling.

Ivan Lumby got up and said, "I do."

Ivan Lumby's shirt was always dirty and half hanging out of his trousers. The zip on his shorts was often undone, and today was no different.

"Do your zip up, Ivan."

Ivan did as he was told to the sound of giggles from the rest of the class.

"Thank you. Now, what are you going to Show and Tell?"

Ivan took out his handkerchief.

"This," said Ivan.

"Go on," said Mr Wallis.

"I want to show my handkerchief," said Ivan Lumby. "It's got my name on it. My mum sewed it in," and he opened out his well-used handkerchief to the 'uurghs' and 'yuchs' of the class.

"Well done, Ivan," said Mr Wallis. "Try to bring something different tomorrow. Who else has a Show and Tell?"

"I do," said Michelle Hutchins. "I brought Princess," and she showed the class her plastic doll. It had only two fingers on one hand and three on the other. Its legs were twisted and it wore a spotted dress decorated with yet more spots of tomato sauce, vinegar, oil and grease. Its hair had nearly all fallen out, leaving only a few very thin golden strands.

"She's got golden hair and blue eyes," said Michelle.

One of Princess's eyes was loose in the socket and rolled around, giving her something of a mad, bad, scary look. The class laughed.

"You shouldn't laugh," said Mr Wallis. "It's not polite."

"But it looks funny, sir," said Brian Evans.

"It's worse than Frankenstein," called out Hermione Lee.

Michelle got angry and kicked Hermione who punched Michelle's legs.

"Stop it! Stop it!" Mr Wallis shouted. "Thank you, Michelle. Look after Princess, won't you."

"Yes, sir. She comes to bed with me every night and she eats at the table with us for supper."

"That's nice. Thank you Michelle."

"And she says 'mama'," Michelle insisted. "Listen!"

She turned Princess upside down making the loose eye roll up to an eyebrow and poked her somewhere near her backside. Princess immediately said in a high, strangled voice something which sounded like 'rubber' but which was supposed to be 'mama'.

"My Katie's much nicer than that," Monica Rich said scornfully. "She cries."

Michelle stuck her tongue out at Monica and sat down.

"Thank you Michelle," said Mr Wallis. "Who else has anything to Show and Tell?"

"Please sir," said Ivan Lumby. "I saw a little man come out of Peotry's calculator."

Peotry jumped. She had taken her calculator out of her bag and put it on her knees, fighting the urge to Show and Tell. She hadn't seen him but Byte might well have poked his head out to see the class.

"I don't think you did," said Mr Wallis getting tired of this Show and Tell which was showing and telling very little. "You shouldn't make up stories, Ivan."

"I'm not making up a story, sir. I did see him. He came out of Peotry's calculator."

Ivan Lumby was not telling a lie. Byte had indeed come out to see what was happening, but went back immediately he saw so many Human Errors around him.

The Show and Tell lesson went on a little bit longer, and Ivan edged closer and closer to Peotry. Suddenly he stuck out his hand and grabbed the calculator.

"Give it back!" cried Peotry. "Give it back! Sir, Ivan's took my calculator. Give it back!"

Ivan held the calculator away from Peotry and shook it around, waiting for the little man to fall out.

"Ivan!" ordered Mr Wallis. "Give it back!"

"Peotry's lying sir," said Ivan. "I did see a little man. He came out and went back in again."

Mr Wallis stood up, took a giant step across the children to Ivan, grabbed the calculator and gave it to Peotry. Peotry, red in the face with anger pinched Ivan hard on his arm and put the calculator away in her bag.

"You mustn't snatch things from other people," said Mr Wallis to everyone, not just to Ivan. "It's wrong. Peotry," he said, trying to make her feel better, "would you like to Show and Tell us about your calculator?"

Peotry shook her head. She hated Ivan Lumby.

"Alright," said Mr Wallis, starting to dread the day ahead. "We'll stop there. Now make sure you listen or you won't know what to do," and he explained to the class what each of the groups would be doing until lunch time.

"Red group, you're going to do leaf prints."

"Again sir?"

"Yes, only properly this time. Green group, you're going to do finger painting."

Green group whispered to each other in delight.

"Yellow group, you're going to do page 35 of your sums."

"Oh no, sir!"

"Don't argue," said Mr Wallis. "White group, you're going to build a robot from cardboard tubes and cereal boxes. Black group, you have to make papier-mâché self-portraits. Orange group, you have to finish your diaries. Purple group, you can use the Lego. Silver group, you use the computer. Blue group, you do your sewing. Violet group, you do a charcoal drawing of a snowman."

Mr Wallis loved his groups.

"Please sir," objected somebody in violet group, "a snowman's white and charcoal's black."

"That's Rayshal Prejadish," someone called out.

"You can get sent to prison for saying that," said another.

"It isn't racial prejudice," said Mr Wallis. "And don't worry violet group about the colours. Think about the shape and the texture. Now that's everyone. Who doesn't know what to do?"

Three children put up their hands.

"Bernie, which group are you in?"

"Don't know, sir."

"You're in the blue group. You do sewing."

"Sewing's for cissies, sir."

"No need to be rude, Bernie. And as it happens, many men are very good at sewing. Elizabeth? What's wrong?"

Elizabeth needed to go to the toilet.

"Patty, which group are you in?"

"Yellow group, sir, but I've done my sums at home."

"Well do some more then, Patty."

"I've finished my book, sir."

"I'll give you another one. Peotry, what do you want?"

"Could I use the computer please, sir?"

"Are you in silver group?"

"No, sir."

"Then you can't. Perhaps after playtime you can use it."

"That's not fair, sir!" cried Elaine. "Why can't I use the computer after play?"

"I said 'maybe'," said Mr Wallis. "Right, enough talk. Go and get on and remember, no mess and no noise."

The class wandered off. Some of the children were unhappy with the work they had to do and wanted to be in different groups. A few of the less friendly ones tore other children's papers or scribbled on their books as they passed by.

It was not going to be an easy morning.

Peotry was in yellow group and sat with her arithmetic book out, staring at page 35. Her calculator lay on the table in front of her and she knew that Ivan Lumby was watching her closely. She leaned over the calculator, pretending to work and whispered,

"Don't come out Byte, it's too dangerous."

To her surprise, the words '*I won't*' appeared on the screen.

Peotry had an idea.

She looked again at page 35. It was full of problems that never happened in real life. For instance, "Tom's pencil is ten centimetres long and Susan's pencil is thirteen centimetres long. How much longer is Susan's pencil than Tom's?"

Peotry leaned over the calculator and read the question in a whisper into it. The sum '$13-10=3$' appeared on the screen and Peotry wrote it down.

She did it again with the next one. It said, "Natasha's book is 25 centimetres wide and Joshua's book is 21 centimetres wide. How much wider is Natasha's book than Joshua's?"

Peotry thought books were supposed to be read, not measured, but she whispered the question into the calculator and up came the answer, $25-21=4$.

Peotry got carried away and did not notice Ivan Lumby standing behind her looking over her shoulder.

"You're a cheat," he said suddenly, and then aloud to everyone, "Peotry's cheating!"

"What's the matter now, Ivan?" Mr Wallis asked.

"Peotry's cheating."

"How is she cheating, Ivan?"

"She's using her calculator."

"That's not cheating," said Mr Wallis. "You can use them if you want."

"But she's talking to it, sir!"

"I'm talking to myself, sir," said Peotry in a moment of inspiration. "If I talk to myself I can think better."

"No she's not sir," insisted Ivan. "She's talking to the calculator and it shows her the answer. It's magic. Peotry's got a magic calculator."

Everyone gasped, always ready to believe in magic. Mr Wallis told Ivan Lumby to get on with his work and leave Peotry alone.

"But sir," insisted Ivan, fighting for truth. "I'm not lying. She's got a magic calculator. It's showing her the answers!"

"Sit down, Ivan."

"But sir!"

"Sit down!"

Ivan sat down, more certain than ever that adults used their bigness rather than their brains and had no idea how to tell truth from lies.

Peotry finished her work normally and had to be very careful as some of the children on her table were now watching her. At one point, the words 'Can I help?' appeared on the calculator screen and Peotry whispered 'No' a little too loud so that some of the group started looking at her in very peculiar ways. When Mr Wallis marked her book, he found all her sums were correct, which for Peotry was most unusual.

"Can I see your calculator?" he asked Peotry.

Peotry took the calculator from her pocket and showed it to Mr Wallis. She was horrified to see on the screen the words, '*Please talk to me.*'

"That's clever," said Mr Wallis.

Luckily for Peotry, his attention was taken by silver group who were squabbling at the computer. He gave the calculator back and called to silver group,

"What's going on?"

"Simon won't let me have a go, sir," cried Tabetha.

"I do, sir," said Simon, "but she wants to use the computer all the time."

"No I don't, sir. *He* does."

"Right," said Mr Wallis. "Peotry, you use the computer. Simon and Tabetha, you get on with your sums."

"Oh, sir!"

Simon and Tabetha grumpily got up as Peotry sat down with Matthew, a boy who had said virtually nothing ever since joining the school. He was using Logo, trying to draw a flower. Peotry looked at the screen and saw a few lines and a few curves, but they were all over the place.

"It doesn't look like a flower," she said, honestly.

Matthew shrugged. Some older children were good at Logo and could make wonderful patterns, but Peotry's class couldn't get it to do much at all except sit and sulk.

Matthew took out a set of picture cards from his pocket and started thumbing through them, ignoring Peotry, so Peotry laid the calculator on the computer table and pressed '*ON*'. She was delighted to see a picture of Byte on the screen. She leaned over, as if to pick up something, and whispered,

"Byte, can you do Logo?"

Byte popped out from the calculator, looked around and then hopped onto the school computer. He stood staring at the screen for a moment, then turned to Peotry, waved and vanished. After a few seconds, the screen cleared and the turtle started moving around, drawing a square.

"I want to draw a flower," said Peotry.

The words '*Do not know how to build Flower*' appeared on the screen.

"Daffodil," whispered Peotry.

Matthew heard Peotry's voice and looked at her, then at the screen, his eyes opening wider and wider.

The turtle was drawing squares, first straight up then turning slightly and drawing another one and so on until a whole series of squares had been drawn making a petal shape. In the middle, the turtle drew a bell. Matthew turned from the masterpiece to Peotry.

"How you do that?" he asked.

"Sshh!" said Peotry.

The turtle was moving again. It was drawing a stalk. The stalk was green and the flower was yellow. A daffodil.

"Nice!" muttered Matthew.

Peotry leaned over, whispered something into the computer and then typed a few instructions. The screen cleared and the daffodil reappeared, much smaller, but over and over again, creating a garden full of identical daffodils.

"Sky," said Peotry. The words '*Do not know how to build Sky*' appeared at the bottom of the screen.

"Never mind," said Peotry, and typed in, 'Build whatever you want, Byte.'

The screen cleared and the turtle began to move by itself, drawing a neat picture of Peotry's computer.

"More," said Peotry.

The screen filled with lots of little computers, all exactly the same.

"You magic," said Matthew to Peotry.

"Build me," said Peotry, and immediately the turtle cleared the screen and filled it with lots of portraits of Peotry.

Had Mr Wallis been an observant teacher he would have seen all this, but he was chasing his tail trying to sort out the finger painters who were not just using their fingers but their hands, elbows, noses, chins and mouths. The junk modellers had cut up the cardboard tubes and cereal boxes but had no idea how to make a robot. The charcoal snowmen had melted into shapeless smudges and the charcoal, like the finger paints, was spreading to faces and clothes. Only the sewing group seemed reasonably clean and happy, away from all the noise.

So Mr Wallis missed the lovely Logo pictures, but Ivan Lumby did not. He had crept up to Peotry and stood behind her.

"You're a witch," he said.

Peotry turned around.

Ivan Lumby was in black group, so his hands were covered in papier-mâché. He was a spiteful boy and determined to get Peotry into trouble.

"Sir," he shouted, "come and look at... ugh!"

Ivan's shout was cut short by a couple of strong fingers pinching his nose. The fingers belonged to Matthew who said threateningly to Ivan, "You shuddup!"

"Lemme go!"

"Shuddup!"

"Get lost!"

"You promise not tell!"

"Promise! Lemme go!"

Matthew let Ivan go. Ivan was about to cry out again to Mr Wallis when he saw Matthew's warning look and was quiet.

"You go!" Matthew said to Ivan.

"I can stand where I want," Ivan replied. Matthew's hand started to twitch and Ivan turned back to his group, sulky and angry.

"Thank you," said Peotry.

"More picture," said Matthew.

Peotry whispered into the computer.

"Byte? Are you there?"

"Byte popped out from the keyboard and sat on the space bar. Matthew's eyes opened wide and he stared in wonder and delight at Byte.

"Who that?" he asked in his odd English.

"That's Byte," said Peotry, "but he's a secret. Please don't tell."

Matthew nodded.

"Can I talk to teacher?" asked Byte.

"Not yet," said Peotry. "He's busy, but it will be playtime in a few minutes. He might stop and talk then. You better go back inside."

Byte nodded and disappeared.

"He gone?" Matthew asked.

"No," said Peotry. "He's hiding."

"I try," said Matthew. He leaned over and whispered, "Draw me."

After a second or two, the turtle started moving. In a few moments there was a complete picture of Matthew on the screen. For the first time since he had been to school, Matthew smiled. "More!" he whispered, and then watched, fascinated, as the turtle drew about fifty Matthews with his big eyes and strong face.

Matthew pointed to the printer then waited as Peotry printed the portrait. Matthew put it inside a large book so that it wouldn't be crinkled and went back to his table to stare at it, entranced, until the bell rang for the end of the lesson.

Peotry waited until everyone had gone. Mr Wallis had been ushering them all out and was desperate for a cup of coffee. Peotry started to say, "Please sir, can I..." but Mr Wallis had swept passed her, into the corridor and the safety of the staffroom.

Peotry muttered something to herself, and then went off to find Beth.

Beth was in the junior school which had a separate playground to the infants, but Beth was so keen to see her sister and find out what happened that she crossed over to talk.

"Well," said Beth. "Did he see him?"

"Who see who?" Peotry asked.

"Did Byte see Mr Wallis?"

"No," said Peotry. "He never got a chance."

"Where is Byte?"

"Safe," said Peotry.

"Can I see him?"

They found a sheltered spot where they could sit down.

"Byte, are you there?"

Byte came out and sat on the plus sign. He looked around and said,

"Your teacher is like me, Peotry, 'Do this, do that'; it will be hard to talk with him."

"I shouldn't bother," said Beth. "He's like that all day, every day. That's why he's called Wally Wallis."

Byte looked puzzled but decided that there were too many puzzling things about The Outside to ask for explanations of them all. Looking around the playground full of running, screaming children he said, "Where are we?"

"This is the infant playground," said Peotry.

"The Infant Playground," repeated Byte. "Is it a country?"

"Of course it isn't," laughed Beth.

"But it is enormous," said Byte, "and there are so many Human Errors."

"You should see the junior playground," said Beth. "It's bigger than this."

"I will," said Byte. "I'll see everything, in time."

Beth asked Byte to come with her. "Please!" and even "Pretty Please!" but Byte would only consider coming if Beth's teacher offered more than Mr Wallis had, which hadn't been very much at all.

"Miss Powell?" Beth wasn't sure, but she didn't say so. "Oh, yes! She's much better, Byte, honestly." Then to Peotry, "Can I take him, just until lunch time? Please!"

Peotry sighed as if she were dealing with a difficult baby sister of her own.

"Oh alright, but don't let him get into trouble and don't lose him."

"Of course I won't!" said Beth.

A new voice suddenly broke up their conversation.

"You're both witches."

Ivan had crept up on them, following Peotry to see what she was up to.

"Who are you?" Beth asked.

"It's Ivan," said Peotry, rolling her eyes.

"I seen him," Ivan said. "You two are witches."

"That's right," said Beth, thinking quickly, "and if you don't go away we'll turn you into a frog with big green spots," and she raised her hand as if about to make some magic gestures. Ivan turned and fled, checking his body to make sure he still had two arms and two legs and that they weren't turning green and bendy.

The whistle blew for the end of play and Peotry said again, "Look after Byte. Don't let him get into trouble."

"I won't," said Beth, and re-joined her class, excitedly.

Beth's class was in the final year of junior school and thought themselves very grown up. Some of them, including Beth, were growing up fast, but quite a few still had a long way to go. One such was Nigel Pole.

"What's that?" he asked Beth, standing beside her in line. Beth had been unable to resist staring at Peotry's calculator.

"Mind your own business, Ni...gel," she said.

She split the word into two because she knew he hated that.

"It's just a cheap baby calculator," he said, then added, "Be...tha...ny."

"It's my sister's, nosey," said Beth. "I'm looking after it for her. So there."

"Pathetic," sneered Nigel. "It's a toy. On mine there's a memory and you can do square roots."

"Who cares about square boots?" said Beth.

"Let me see it," Nigel said.

"No."

"Go on. I won't break it."

"No."

The line of children snaked on and up into Beth's classroom. They were going to do a mental arithmetic test and Nigel took out his fancy scientific calculator with lots of mysterious symbols on it and proudly laid it on the table.

"Better than yours," he said to Beth. "Yours is a baby's."

"This is *mental* arithmetic," she said. "That means in your *head*, stupid."

"I'm good at any kind of arithmetic," said Nigel Pole. "My father is a tax inspector and he's excellent at figures."

Nigel had a pompous way of talking that made Beth want to drop him head first from the school roof.

"He gives me arithmetic lessons every day and checks my work," said Nigel. "He doesn't think teachers are particularly clever."

"Oh, doesn't he?" mimicked Beth. "He sounds more stuck up than you."

"No calculators for this," Miss Powell said. "Heads only."

There was a rare silence in the class as all the children struggled with tricky problems that made their brains hurt, but Beth, being bright, scored higher than Nigel.

"Is your father a tax inspector too?" he asked, impressed and jealous at the same time.

"I don't know what that means," said Beth. "Does he clean taxis or something?"

"A tax inspector collects money that people owe the government," said Nigel. "It's very clever work. My father is a highly intelligent man."

Beth looked up to heaven, impatient to talk with Byte and see him in action again.

Miss Powell told the class to begin their written arithmetic work and that they could use their calculators from then on, if they wanted. Beth put her head into her satchel and whispered, "Byte? Are you there?"

No answer.

"Byte? Byte?"

Nothing.

"Are you alright, Beth?" Miss Powell asked anxiously, seeing Beth doubled up on her chair with her head in her bag, thinking that she might be sick.

"Fine, miss," Beth replied.

"Sit up properly then," said Miss Powell.

Beth sat up and tapped the calculator, hoping to see a picture of Byte or something to say he was there, but the calculator remained quiet and Beth started to experience a horrible sinking feeling.

She tried to concentrate on her arithmetic but was growing edgy, not knowing what she could tell Peotry if Byte had vanished.

Shortly before lunch, Miss Powell sat with Beth's group to see what they were doing. She checked each of the books in turn and praised Nigel's but not Beth's. Beth was normally up there with the best of them but had become so worried about losing Byte that she'd hardly done anything.

"Long multiplication," said Miss Powell. "Thirty three times twenty four. Do it in your books. Nigel, you needn't do it if you don't want to."

"I don't mind, miss. My father says it's good for me to practise."

Bill Bullen, a boy who didn't suffer fools gladly, mimicked him. *"My father said..."* Nigel went red.

When they were all stumped, Miss Powell took out her pen to show them the correct method and then her own calculator to check the answer, but instead of seeing figures on the screen, she saw - and everyone at the table saw - a tiny, puzzled face staring up at them.

"My goodness!" exclaimed Miss Powell. "What's that?"

"It must be a bug," said Nigel, "or a virus. My father says viruses can get into computers like they can get into people and make them ill."

Miss Powell tried again but up came the same tiny face. Beth was relieved because she knew at once where Byte was. But how had he got there? He must have popped out of her calculator and across to Miss Powell's bag! She had to get him back!

Miss Powell shook the calculator. She switched it off and on again. She checked the batteries. Everything she tried, back came the tiny face. Then the face disappeared and up came the words 'Can you answer my questions?' Miss Powell dropped the calculator as if it was red hot and Beth tried to grab it, but Nigel Pole got there first.

"It's definitely a virus," he said. "You'll have to get an anti-virus program."

"For a calculator?" asked Miss Powell, astonished and flustered.

"My father says they get everywhere," said Nigel. "This one is an ugly one."

The words on the screen disappeared and the face appeared again, this time with the tongue sticking out. Presumably at Nigel. Bill laughed.

"I think it can hear you," he said.

The other children in the class, hearing the disturbance came over to see what was happening. Nigel put the calculator down in the middle of the table and said aloud,

"It's a virus. It gets into computers and makes programs go wrong."

"Can it get into people as well?" someone asked.

"No, my father says..."

"Oh, shut up about your father," interrupted Beth. "What does he know about computers anyway?"

And on the screen of Miss Powell's calculator appeared the word, "*Nothing*".

"It's a very clever virus," said Nigel.

"It's not a virus, you idiot," said Beth, "it's..."

"It's what?" asked Bill.

"It's me!" appeared on the calculator screen. The children screamed with delight.

"You could ask it questions, miss," said Bonnie Holdstock, a bright girl with big, bold eyes. "Ask what its name is."

"I can't talk to a calculator!" said Miss Powell. "That's silly!"

"I'll do it," said Bonnie. "Calculator, what's your name?"

The word '*Anon*' appeared.

"Told you miss," said Bonnie. "The bug's name is Anon."

"Anon means anonymous," said Miss Powell, starting to sweat a little. "It doesn't want to tell."

"Secret," appeared on the screen.

"What do you want?" Bonnie called out.

"Answers."

"What's the question?" Bonnie said.

Question marks started appearing all over the screen.

"I think it's got lots of questions," said Bonnie Holdstock.

"This is ridiculous!" said Miss Powell who was of a nervous disposition at the best of times and was beginning to wonder whether she'd been a teacher for too long.

Beth was red with embarrassment. Whatever questions Byte wanted answered, this wasn't the way to do it. But Bonnie Holdstock had become over-excited and was determined to get to the bottom of things.

"Are you a bug?" she called out.

"No," came the reply. Then, "Are you?" Everyone laughed.

"Are you a virus?" asked Bonnie.

"No."

"What are you then?" Bonnie said.

"Secret," appeared on the screen.

"Are you alive?" Bonnie asked.

"Some expected 'yes', others 'no'. But instead, out popped a little creature with an inquisitive face and stood staring at them on the minus sign of the calculator, his eyes the most wonderfully sharp pin pricks of curiosity.

Someone screamed.

Unfortunately, it was Miss Powell.

And then someone fainted.

Also Miss Powell.

Silence, then gasps.

"Go and get a teacher!" shouted Bonnie. "Go on!"

Someone went out into the corridor to call for help. One or two of the more nervous children backed away and suddenly there was a lot of pushing and shoving. In the chaos, Beth lost sight of Byte and called out,

"Don't push! Don't push! You'll squish him! Don't push!"

Mr Loveday, the Headmaster, came in, ushered everyone out and, with the help of some other teachers, carried Miss Powell to the staffroom. She rambled on about talking calculators and little creatures but they assumed this was because she wasn't well.

Inside the classroom, Beth remained behind as long as possible looking here, there and everywhere, but it was no use.

Byte was gone.

Bit 3: A World Of Knowledge

"Lost?" cried Peotry. "It's not true!"

"I'm really sorry," said Beth. "We'll find him again Peotry, honest. It wasn't my fault."

"You lost him! You lost him!" cried Beth.

"I didn't mean to," said Beth, almost in tears herself. "I'm sure we'll find him again."

"We'll never find him!" cried Peotry. "He's so small and the school is so big! It's dangerous. Someone will tread on him and he'll be killed!"

Beth was forlorn. Peotry was probably right, Byte was bound to be hurt in this big, noisy, careless school.

But Byte was not in danger.

In fact he found the world of Human Errors very slow, and when the need arose he could move far faster than anything on The Outside.

During the chaos in Beth's class, Byte had hidden himself in Bonnie Holdstock's bag. Bonnie spent most of her lunchtimes in the library, and that day was no exception. So

Byte peeked out of Bonnie's bag to find himself in a world of knowledge. Bonnie went over to the librarian and put her bag down on the table next to the computer. Byte whizzed into it. Bonnie returned some books and then went away to sit somewhere quietly and read.

Byte quickly found his way around. He couldn't read the writing of Human Errors, but he understood the meaning of things in his own way and soon knew the titles of all the books in the library. He even found 'Jack and the Beanstalk' and 'Cinderella'. But knowing these things didn't satisfy him.

"There must be more to books than names," he said to himself, "just as there is more to Byte than Byte and more to Peotry Willow than Peotry Willow."

Saying Peotry's name made him wonder for a moment about his new friend, but because he had never known friendship, only rules, he didn't understand what it was to worry about somebody else or for someone else to worry about him.

In his excitement at being near so much knowledge, he forgot his wish for secrecy and popped out, just as the librarian was about to type something into the computer.

"Good gracious!" exclaimed the librarian, a little Scottish lady who had seen a lot of the world, but nothing like Byte. "What's this?"

Byte looked around to see what 'this' was, then realized that it was him.

"I'm Byte," he said.

"Are you, indeed?" replied the librarian, keeping her presence of mind. "And what may that be?"

"Nothing," said Byte, "except me."

"And what are you doing on my computer?"

"I was learning the titles of all the books," said Byte.

"All?" asked the librarian.

Byte nodded.

"Two thousand, four hundred and thirty six," he said.

"That many?" said the librarian, impressed. "And why would you need the titles of all my books?"

"Because I want to learn," said Byte, "about Human Errors and The Outside. Are they really all *your* books?" he asked.

"Figure of speech," replied the librarian. "I look after them, but they are not, strictly speaking, all mine."

"Do you know what's in them?" Byte asked.

"Some," the librarian said, modestly.

"Will you tell me?" Byte asked. "I'm a good listener."

"Have you any particular book in mind?" asked the librarian.

"No," said Byte. "Choose one."

"I think, first, you ought to tell me who you are," said the librarian. "I can't reveal such secrets to anyone."

"I told you," said Byte. "I'm Byte."

"And where do you come from, Byte?"

"From Peotry Willow's computer," said Byte. "That's my home."

"Ah," said the librarian. "Peotry Willow is in the infants, isn't she?"

"She lives in The Infant Playground," said Byte.

"Lives there! I hope not," said the librarian. "What are you doing here, Byte?"

"It's a long story," Byte replied, "though it isn't really a story because it's true. Peotry brought me to school because I wanted to talk to Mr Wally but he was too busy so I went to Beth's class to talk to her teacher but she screamed and died..."

"Died!"

"Well she closed her eyes and fell over when she saw me," said Byte.

"Mm," said the librarian.

"Then there were lots of Human Errors running around so I hid in that girl's bag and here I am."

"Here you are, indeed," said the librarian. "And now you are here, you want me to tell you about all these books? I would like to, but I'm afraid I can't, you sweet little creature. I am a busy lady, you know, Byte."

"All Human Errors say they are busy," said Byte, "but they don't run around half as much as me. What do you have to do?"

"I have new books to enter, old books to delete, records to check, reminders to send out, letters to write..."

"I can help," said Byte. "Tell me what to do and I'll do it, then you must open up your world of knowledge for me."

"Alright," said the librarian, wondering what the tiny creature could possibly mean. "You scratch my back and I'll scratch yours."

Byte looked horrified at the idea, but assumed it was a Human Error way of speaking.

"What shall I do?" he asked. "Show me."

The librarian explained to Byte about all the records of all the books and how they had to be changed. Certain numbers had to be given new numbers and moved to new places in the computer. Those with other numbers had to be given still different numbers and put somewhere else. Books with tagged numbers had to be taken off the computer altogether as they were marked down as old and were going to be sold. Other books were overdue and reminders had to be sent to the borrowers to tell them to return their books. The librarian's jobs went on and on until she said,

"But that will do. I can't tell you everything."

"No problem," Byte said. "Is that all?"

"That's enough," came the reply. "Let's see what you can do," she added, not really believing that the odd little fellow could do anything at all.

Byte dropped into the computer and disappeared.

The librarian watched as numbers raced around the screen, faster and faster. She thought she might see smoke coming from it, things were on the move so quickly. No more than five minutes later, the printer sprang into life, printing lists and addresses, after which Byte popped out.

"All done," he said.

"All?" asked the librarian.

"Unless there's more?" Byte asked.

The librarian shook her head.

"You're a very useful little chap to have around," she said. "You've probably saved me a few weeks work."

"That's good," said Byte. "Now you must scratch my back."

The librarian laughed and said,

"Let me think. Yes, I know."

She fetched a large atlas of the world and laid it open on the desk.

"What is it?" Byte asked.

"Maps," said the librarian. "Maps of all the countries in the world."

"They are beautiful colours," said Byte. "Do you think you could sit me somewhere higher where I could see better, please?"

The librarian carefully lifted Byte onto the top of the monitor. Byte looked down as the librarian turned the pages of the atlas, telling Byte what they were looking at. Had anyone seen her, they might have thought her rather odd, talking to herself like that, but she had always been considered a little eccentric.

She showed Byte the countries of the world, the continents, the oceans, the seas, the mountain ranges, the deserts and the big cities, the forests, the tundra, the Steppes, the islands, the wildernesses and the civilisations.

"Which country am I in?" Byte asked. "Is it the country of The Infant Playground?"

"England," said the librarian, "in the continent of Europe."

"But that's yellow. And here is not yellow."

The librarian explained to Byte what a map was, or tried to, but it was very difficult to explain anything to a creature that had spent all its life pushing particles around in the quantum world and had never seen the sky or the sun.

"Is the sky close?" Byte asked, looking up.

"Very close and very far," the librarian said. "Ask Peotry to show it to you. And the sun. And the sky at night. You will like the sky at night."

"Can you put me in England?" Byte asked, and the librarian put Byte in England.

"Where in England am I?" Byte asked.

"In London," said the librarian.

"Will you put me in London?"

The librarian put Byte in London.

"Where in London am I?" Byte asked.

"North of the River Thames," the librarian said, "but I can't show you exactly. The map is too small."

"It is much too small. It doesn't show the library or Peotry Willow's house or The Infant Playground or the bits in between. But it shows the whole world. How strange!"

"The world is very big," said the librarian. "You cannot put it all into a book. Or even a thousand books."

"A thousand is not many," said Byte.

"Alright, a million books. You couldn't put the world even into a million books."

"Then why do you try?" Byte asked.

"You ask difficult questions," said the librarian, "which shows you are very clever. I wish I was clever enough to answer them."

"I wonder who is," moaned Byte. "Peotry's teacher has no time and he is a Wally..."

"I beg your pardon?"

"Wally Wallis." Byte said, innocently. "That's what they call him."

"Do they, indeed?"

"Yes they do. Then Beth's teacher went funny on me and now your atlas is too small. Who shall I ask?" he sighed. "I want to be wise. I want to know True Wisdom."

"Ask everyone," said the librarian. "Look, listen, learn. You can't hurry such things."

"But I am used to speed," said Byte. "I'm not good at doing things slowly."

"Perhaps I can help a little," said the librarian, lifting Byte off the monitor and taking him to another computer. "Do you know what this is?" she asked.

"No," said Byte.

"It's called a CD ROM," said the librarian.

"A seedy room?" Byte asked.

"It can tell us lots of things about the world in pictures and sounds. All I have to do is put in the drive, like this, and it's ready to go."

"Shall I get inside?" Byte asked.

"As long as you don't damage it, aye, I suppose you can."

"Trust me," Byte said, and he disappeared into the CD ROM. Pictures and sounds flashed over the screen, a blur of colour and sound. A few minutes later Byte popped out.

"That was good," he said. "I think I'm a little wiser now."

The librarian was quickly growing fond of her tiny new pupil. He had a thirst for knowledge which was, she thought, quite rare.

"So what was it all about?" she asked, intrigued.

"It was about The Outside," said Byte.

"Everything is about The Outside, as you call it," said the librarian, "in a way."

"It was about evolution," Byte said, proud of a good, long word, "about people becoming Human Errors from monkeys. But that is a puzzle. I have always been me. It is hard to think of changing from one kind of creature to another."

"It takes a long time," said the librarian.

"Millions of years," said Byte, "but I was still Byte, even then."

"Were you?" the librarian asked, surprised. "Were there computers so long ago?"

"Not in the same way," said Byte. "But The Power has always been around."

"What power?" asked the librarian.

"The Power you take from a hole in the wall."

The librarian had to think for a moment before the truth dawned.

"You mean electricity," she said. "Ah, I see. Or I think I see. Human beings have only used electricity for a hundred years or so, Byte. We didn't know about it before then, but I suppose you are right, it was there nevertheless. Now, my little friend, I have an idea."

She searched through a shelf full of CDs and took out another one.

"This is all about electricity. Why don't you take a peek? It may help you some way towards, erm, True Wisdom."

"That's a very good idea," said Byte.

The librarian put the disk in the drive and Byte hurried into the machine.

"Be careful," said the librarian, still worried in case her seedy room should get damaged.

Lights, colours and sounds sped by on the screen and in a few minutes Byte popped out. There was a radiant look on his face.

"That was most interesting," he said, "most interesting!"

"Is electricity... The Power?" asked the librarian.

Byte cocked his head to one side, thinking. After a moment he said,

"Maybe. Part of it. You have had to learn so much, whereas I just know what I know. You knew nothing and you learned. That must be difficult. I feel very humble."

The librarian laughed.

"Would you like to see it again?" she asked.

"Again?" Byte asked. "Why should I see it again? I have seen it and I know it. There would be no point in seeing it again."

"Sometimes we Human Errors like to do things more than once," said the librarian, "because, well, we enjoy them. They give us pleasure."

"Hmm," said Byte. "Interesting. I have never thought in that way. Alright. I will see it again."

Byte jumped into the CD ROM and settled down to enjoy the second learning, but his enjoyment was cut short by the unexpected entrance of Mr Loveday, the Headmaster.

"Is it ready, Mrs McNee?"

"Ready, Mr Loveday?"

Mrs McNee looked bewildered. Bells were beginning to ring. Evidently the surprise of dealing with Byte had pushed something important out of her normally organised and reliable head.

"The CD ROM?" Mr Loveday reminded her. "I booked it for the assembly this afternoon?"

"Oh my! Mr Loveday, I'm so sorry. I've been having a very... well... oh dear!"

"What's the matter, Mrs McNee?"

"Could you come back for it in a few minutes, Mr Loveday?" asked the flustered librarian. "I'll get it ready for you."

"No, no, don't worry, Mrs McNee. I'll do it myself. These things are very simple to set up. I'll switch it off first... there. Unplug it... done! And ready to go! Thank you, Mrs McNee."

"Oh dear," said the librarian, and then to herself, "Poor Byte!"

Byte knew something had happened and popped out to see. He saw the rather fierce face of Mr Loveday and immediately went back inside. He was impatient to renew his enjoyment of learning a second time around. However, when The Power returned, everything was different.

Byte looked out from beneath the space bar of the computer keyboard. In front of him were hundreds of Human Errors, sitting down in rows, staring up at the man who had been carrying him. He had, compared to any Human Error Byte had heard so far, a thunderous voice. Byte decided it wasn't a good time to re-enter The Outside and disappeared again into the CD ROM.

"That is not the way to come into assembly!" bellowed Mr Loveday, red-faced and angry. Mr Loveday was often red-faced and angry. His ambition in life had been to be an actor, and he had tried but failed. Instead of playing to packed, appreciative adult audiences, he played to packed, unappreciative children. Life was unfair.

In the audience, Peotry was edgy. She never liked Friday afternoon assemblies, they were too crowded. All years from one to six were there, and she didn't enjoy being squashed like a sardine, but most of all Mr Loveday scared her. She thought he was always about to explode into a thousand tiny bits all over the Hall. Today was worse because her careless sister had lost Byte.

"I've a mind to send you all out and we'll enter the Hall again in absolute silence," roared Mr Loveday. Byte felt the circuits rattle where he was hiding. He did not like this Human Error with the scary voice. He did not want to be found by him. But at the same time, he had seen his friend Peotry's face amongst the other Human Errors and wanted to catch her attention.

"This afternoon we are going to learn about global warming," said Mr Loveday. A murmur of disappointment spread through the hall, especially where the top juniors were sitting. Many of them had studied global warming in class projects, seen all about it on television, read about it in comics, done drama about it, written stories and composed poems and songs about it. Still it never seemed to be done and they never seemed to understand what it was all about. Why didn't grown-ups, if they were so clever, just spray the air with something to make it colder?

Mr Loveday had decided to give it another go.

"Global warming is important..." he said, but neither Peotry nor Beth were listening.

'Oh where is he?' Peotry worried.

I hope he's alright,' thought Beth. 'I bet he'd know about global warming. He could probably stop it in five minutes.'

"Global warming is speeding up," said Mr Loveday, "and will take years to slow down. If we do not stop it the Earth will become like Venus, a burning hot fire raining sulphuric acid."

'Won't the rain put out the fire?' thought Peotry, imagining the school and her house in flames. Oh, where was Byte?

"This CD ROM will tell you about global warming, but first we are going to have some drama from 6K."

6K was the class next to Beth's. They always seemed to be doing drama. This time the drama was a mime so it was left up to the audience to decide what it was all about. Some of the class represented aerosols, some were pollutants, some fossil fuels, others clouds and rays of ultra violet light from the sun. The sun was a spotty boy called Colin Dicks who spent the whole time gently waving his arms to represent flames and then turning to represent... turning. The Earth was Monica Mason who gradually wilted from a tall and healthy planet to a poor, melted mess. Heat rays from the sun kept bombarding the Earth but were unable to escape, held back by the pollution, fossil fuels and aerosols. In all, the Earth had a hard time of it and in the end gave up the fight and died to a round of applause from the audience. Peotry clapped too, though she had no idea what had been going on; she had just liked all the movement and strange contortions, especially Monica Mason curling up in agonies and falling in a heap to the ground.

"And now the CD ROM!" said the headmaster, keen to show off his skills with new technology. CDs were more common than pencil and paper, but the audience humoured Mr Loveday by looking excited. Fortunately, it was a good one with simple explanations and colourful pictures. Mr Loveday clicked the mouse with care and great self-importance.

"Here is a diagram of normal atmospheric conditions," said Mr Loveday. "If I click here you will see a close up of each part of the picture. You, girl, in front. What is this?"

"The sun, sir," said Girl.

"And you, boy. What is this?"

"The atmosphere," said Boy.

"Very good. And now..."

'Oh Byte!' Peotry was thinking while Mr Loveday talked. 'Where are you? Please don't be dead. Please!'

"If I click on this button," said Mr Loveday with great authority, "we see the emissions from a factory. Boy, what does emissions mean?"

"Don't know sir," said Boy.

"You, girl. What does emissions mean?"

"It means to leave out sir," said Girl.

"No it does not!" said Mr Loveday, his voice rising against such ignorance. "That is Omission. Emissions means waste gasses escaping into the ...? Yes?"

"Atmosphere!" everyone said.

"That's right. Now, if I click here you will see a different kind of emission."

Mr Loveday clicked, fully expecting to see a hand pressing the button of an aerosol. Instead, there was just the picture of a little man, waving with both hands, like a stuck robot, to the audience.

Peotry almost jumped for joy. So did Beth, and she looked at Peotry to warn her to be still, but Peotry was staring at the screen. She knew that Byte was waving to her and she couldn't help but wave back. This might have drawn attention to her, but it didn't because everyone was waving.

Mrs McNee had crept into the hall, hoping against hope that everything would go smoothly and sighed with resignation when she saw Byte on the screen.

Miss Powell, who was just recovering from the shock of the morning, gave a shriek and sat motionless, her hand covering her mouth.

Mr Loveday clicked on another button and the face disappeared.

"Some computer programs are not one hundred percent bug free," he said, trying to show off his knowledge of computers and to reassure his audience that everything was under control. "Now, if I click here, we should get some moving pictures of ultra violet rays leaving the sun and hitting the atmosphere. Oh my!"

The moving pictures had started out well, but suddenly from the clouds in the lower atmosphere there started to fall lots of tiny figures, like space invaders, all waving. Instantly the school began to wave back. Mr Loveday clicked on a few buttons until the screen was normal again.

"There are bugs in the program," he said. "Nothing to laugh or be silly about."

The school went quiet, but everyone knew that they would laugh and wave again if the little man showed his face.

"We'll try once more," said Mr Loveday. "Now, here we have some moving pictures to explain what's happening in the sky which is gradually destroying the ozone. You, boy. What is ozone?"

"Ozone protects us from the harmful rays of the sun," said Boy, who in this case was Nigel Pole sounding as much as possible like his father.

"Very good," said Mr Loveday. "Well done. Now watch what happens to the ozone when it mixes with these other chemicals that we produce. I'll just click here…"

He clicked, and the chemicals from the Earth mixed with the ozone of the atmosphere to produce… hundreds of tiny, smiling figures, waving away. Beth and Peotry and the rest of the school waved back in good fellowship, but Mr Loveday turned bright red with anger and clicked on the 'END' button.

"These infernal machines!" he said to himself, his confidence completely gone. "Alright, everybody. Quiet. Quiet! We'll sing a song together," said Mr Loveday. "Hopefully nothing can go wrong with this. Lord of the Dance, Mrs Preston, please."

Mrs Preston, the music teacher, led the school into the song.

Now Mr Loveday had not turned off the CD ROM, but left the END message of the program, thinking that if he didn't press any buttons, nothing could happen.

But it did.

Halfway through Lord of the Dance the screen started to dissolve and a message in giant letters formed on the screen.

"Hello Peotry Willow!"

it said. Then it faded and returned as,

"Hello Beth Willow!"

The school stopped singing and gasped. Everyone turned to look at Peotry and Beth who both went red with embarrassment. Only Mr Loveday carried on singing because he had not seen the messages. When he turned to look, the messages vanished, and instead was a full screen picture of the 'space invader' man, waving at the school with the school waving back.

Mr Loveday turned off the CD ROM determined to telephone the makers of "Global Warming - The CD" and claim all his money back. He dismissed the school in a fierce temper.

Mrs McNee stayed behind to take the CD ROM back to the library. She also called on Peotry and Beth Willow to help.

Once they were alone, Mrs McNee faced the two sisters.

"Do you want him back?" she asked.

Peotry and Beth looked at each other.

"You know?" asked Beth.

Mrs McNee nodded.

"I met him," she said, "a charming wee man."

"Is that good?" asked Byte, climbing out of the CD ROM over the 'K' key, hopping down to the 'M' and onto the space bar where he sat down.

"Oh, Byte!" said Peotry. "I'm so glad you're alive!"

"And I'm glad you're alive, too," said Byte.

"Of course, I'm alive," said Peotry. "It's you that was lost."

"Was I?" asked Byte.

"You're a little baby," said Beth. "We'll have to watch you all the time."

"He's a clever little baby, though," said Mrs McNee.

"Babies are new to the world," said Byte. "I have learned that. And I am not new. I have been here forever. How can I be a baby?"

"We'll tell you when we get home," said Beth.

"Let's go now," said Peotry, "before anything else happens."

"It will," said Mrs McNee. "You can't have a wee fellow like Byte around and not expect trouble."

"You won't tell?" asked Beth.

"Me? Och, no," said Mrs McNee. "But he's told the whole school already!"

"And Ivan Lumby knows," said Peotry. "And Matthew."

"And Bonnie Holdstock and Nigel Pole and most of my class," said Beth.

"So I'm not a secret anymore?" Byte asked.

Peotry shook her head, then said, "Come on, Byte. Get into my calculator. I'll take you home and I'll read you a new story."

"Excellent," said Byte. "This has been an interesting day but I am looking forward to my daffodil bed."

Relieved and happy, Beth took Peotry's hand and they made their way home. Byte curled up inside a vacant memory cell, trying to remember everything he had learned on his path to True Wisdom.

She fetched a large atlas of the world and laid it open on the desk.

Bit 4: Near Disaster

"So there you are," said Peotry. "That's the story of 'The Snow Queen'."

Byte was very quiet, thinking about the tale he had just been told.

"Did you like it?" asked Beth. She and Peotry were sitting on the floor. Between them was the daffodil in which Byte was resting and listening.

"I think I understand the story," Byte said. "There must be a Human Error word for how it makes me feel, because I do not feel like Byte at the moment."

Byte sensed that the words had changed him, but he didn't know how. He felt little warm, wet blobs leaking from his eyes and running down his cheeks.

"You're sad," said Peotry. "Stories can make you feel that way."

Byte wiped away the tears, hoping he wasn't going to leak forever.

There had been a good deal of ice in the story so he asked Beth and Peotry if he could see some. Beth brought in two small cubes of refrigerator ice in a tumbler. Byte climbed onto the edge of the tumbler and then jumped down. The cubes were like icebergs next to him but Byte didn't even shiver.

"Ice is still," he said, "but there are stiller things in The Inside World. How did you make it?"

"It's frozen water," said Beth. "On hot days you can put ice in drinks and it cools you down."

"I should not like to be a Human Error," said Byte, "putting such a thing as ice inside me."

"It doesn't hurt," said Peotry.

"Is it possible," Byte asked, "in The Outside World to turn a Human Error's heart to ice?"

But they were too young to know the answer.

Byte touched the ice cubes.

"Don't you feel cold?" Beth asked.

Byte shook his head.

"It is just still," he said.

As he touched the cubes, drops of water began to fall.

"Be careful," warned Beth.

"I can get inside," said Byte, "and warm it. Shall I?"

"You'll freeze to death," Beth said.

"I won't," Byte replied, and the next second he was gone. When he wanted, Byte was very, very fast. Beth and Peotry watched in awe as the ice began to melt.

"He'll drown," cried Peotry.

Beth thought the same thing, but hardly had they time to think the thought when something strange began happening to the water in the tumbler.

Bubbles began to rise from the bottom to the top.

Faster and faster.

"It's turning to steam!" Beth cried in amazement.

Sure enough, the water was boiling and within a few seconds steam began rising.

"It's magic!" exclaimed Peotry.

The girls watched the water bubble away until all that was left at the bottom of the tumbler was...

"Byte!" Peotry called. "You're not frozen!"

"Not drowned! Not melted!" Beth exclaimed.

"I'm fine," said Byte. "Stirring up my brothers and sisters, that's all. Good exercise!"

"You're magic!" Peotry exclaimed.

"No," said Byte. "Magic breaks rules and that can't happen, although I have learned that in your world, rules are not the same as mine. They are bendable."

Ryan appeared at the door looking both sheepish and intrigued.

"Can I come in?" he asked.

Peotry grabbed her beloved big brother's hand and pulled him inside. Ryan lifted Peotry up to the ceiling, whirling her round. Peotry laughed, but Byte's tiny eyes opened wide.

"What are you doing?" he cried in alarm.

"Having fun," Ryan answered. "Besides, I've got two sisters. If I drop this one, I've still got another one."

"That's true," said Byte, seriously, "but why did you do it?"

Ryan put Peotry down and said gently,

"She's my little sister and I love her. She likes being whirled around, so I do it."

"I like it too," said Beth.

"You're too big" Ryan said. "Did you have a good day at school? Did you get to talk with Wally Wallis?"

"No," said Byte. "He was very busy."

"I'll bet he was," said Ryan.

"You should have seen what Byte did!" said Peotry. "He got into the computer and drew these fantastic pictures."

"And into Miss Powell's calculator," said Beth. "She fainted!"

"And then he got into the assembly computer," Peotry said, laughing, "and waved to the school and we all waved back and Mr Loveday got angry."

"Everyone saw him," said Beth. "Byte's not really a secret anymore."

"In that case," said Ryan, "will you come to my school? It's more grown up than theirs."

"I would like to go to the library," said Byte, "and see some more atlases."

"I've got an atlas," said Peotry, "but it's round, not flat." Byte looked puzzled. "Look," said Peotry, and showed him a globe of the world mounted on a plastic model of the ancient god Atlas.

"What is that?" Byte asked.

"It's the world," answered Peotry.

"But the librarian showed me flat countries in a flat book," said Byte. "The Outside is a mystery to me," he sighed, "just like The Inside is a mystery to you."

"This is where we are," Beth explained, taking the globe and pointing to England. "This is France. This is the North Pole. This is the South Pole. And these are all the continents. Af…."

"Who is the man?" Byte interrupted, looking at the muscled body holding up the world.

"That's Atlas," said Ryan. "A long time ago they thought he was a god who held up the Earth."

"Does he?" Byte asked.

"Of course not," Beth answered. "The Earth turns round in space and it goes around the sun. Nothing holds it up."

"And it doesn't fall down?" Byte asked.

"No," said Beth, "because… it just doesn't."

"Gravity," Ryan said. "Gravity keeps it spinning around the sun, just like the other planets."

"Other planets?" Byte asked, dazzled by all this mysterious talk.

"Mercury, Venus, Earth, Mars, Jupiter, Saturn, Neptune, Uranus, Pluto. The planets. They all go around the sun."

"The Outside is beginning to sound like The Inside," said Byte, "but I still don't understand its bendy rules."

"That makes two of us," said Ryan. "Wish I did."

"Here," said Beth, taking the globe. "I'll teach you some more countries," and she launched into a lightning tour of Earth. "These blue bits..."

"Are the seas and oceans," said Byte.

"You're quick," said Ryan.

"Lightning fast," said Beth who showed off as much as she knew until she ran out of knowledge.

"You should have seen what he did just now!" Peotry said to Ryan, proud of her amazing little friend. "He made ice cubes melt and then he made the water boil and there was steam. He did it all by himself."

Ryan couldn't see how this was possible.

"He did," Beth said. "Byte can do anything."

"No," said Byte. "I can only follow rules. That is my skill and my... sadness."

"Not sad," said Ryan. "I wish I could follow rules like that."

Another figure appeared at the door.

Mr Willow stood there, holding a letter in his hand, looking at his three children and especially at Byte.

"Still here?" asked Mr Willow, rather shy of this stranger in their house.

"Of course," Peotry said. "He's come to stay, haven't you Byte?"

"For a while," Byte replied, "until I know enough. Then I'll go back."

Mr Willow came in and asked about school, if there were any problems and whether or not Byte had learned much.

"I did," said Byte, "but not from Peotry's teacher, nor Beth's. I learned most from Mrs McNee."

"The librarian," explained Peotry. "You should have seen..." and they told their father all the things that had happened. They thought he would have been delighted, and he was, but he also looked rather preoccupied, as if he couldn't concentrate totally on what they were saying.

"What's the matter, Dad?" asked Ryan. "Something up?"

"Yes. This problem at work," said Mr Willow. "It's getting serious."

"Can I help?" Byte asked.

"If only you could," said Mr Willow. "But this is all to do with money."

"Too much or too little?" asked Ryan.

"Too little," said Mr Willow. "The figures don't add up. Big headache. I'll have to go into work tomorrow morning and try to sort it all out."

"Let me come too," Ryan said. "Two heads are better than one, Dad."

"And me," Beth said.

"And me," added Peotry.

"No," said Mr Willow. "Ryan, you can come if you like. Beth and Peotry, sorry, another time."

"May I go?" Byte asked. "I would be most interested."

Mr Willow looked relieved. He'd been hoping the little creature would offer his help, though he wasn't sure exactly what Byte might do.

"If you like," Mr Willow said, awkwardly, not wanting to hope too much. The problem was serious and difficult to solve.

"What's the letter about, Dad?" Ryan asked, seeing his father fiddling with it like it was a piece of hot potato.

"Money," said Mr Willow. "Isn't it always? It's from a tax inspector, Mr Pole."

Peotry's ears pricked up.

"Pole?" Beth repeated. "I bet that's Nigel Pole's father! He's a boy in my class," she explained. "He's always going on about his father. 'My father says this, my father says that'. Gets on my nerves."

"I will look at the inside of your problem," said Byte. "An answer may be clearer there." Mr Willow prayed that it would be. "But I need help from you, Peotry. Let me sit on your hand... yes, good; now please lower me to the Point of Power."

"He means the mains socket in the wall," said Ryan. "Is that safe, Byte?" he asked.

"For me," said Byte. "Not for you. The hole in the wall is where The Power lives."

"No one lives..." Peotry was about to say, of course, that no one lived there, but Ryan tapped her on the shoulder and put his finger to his mouth.

Peotry gently lowered Byte until he was level with the socket. Byte stood up and with a look of wonder and expectation stared into it.

"Closer," he said.

"That's close enough Peotry," warned Mr Willow.

Byte jumped into the 'Live' slot, his little arms stretched out sideways, holding on to the edges of the plastic, keeping his balance.

"Be careful!" Peotry said. "You heard what daddy said. It's dangerous!"

Byte peered in, but didn't disappear, and when he turned around, there was a look of puzzlement on his face.

"What's the matter?" Peotry asked.

"It isn't what I expected," said Byte.

"What were you expecting?" asked Mr Willow.

"The Power," Byte answered.

"But it is there," said Beth. "If you plug something in and switch on, you get power."

Mr Willow explained that electric power didn't actually come from any particular hole in the wall, it came from power stations, often a long way away.

"Like railway stations?" asked Peotry.

"Not quite," said Mr Willow. "Power doesn't stop there, it starts there. People make it."

"Human Errors cannot make power!" Byte objected. "The Power makes Human Errors."

"I don't think so," said Mr Willow. "At least, that's not how I understand it."

"Nor I," said Byte. "This is confusing. I must go to one of these Stations of Power and see. Will you take me?"

"I can't right now," replied Mr Willow. "The main ones are far away. It would take too long to get there."

"And they wouldn't let you in," warned Ryan. "Power Stations are dangerous. You can get killed."

"The Power can't kill," Byte said, astonished. "The Power gives life."

"Not if you touch a hundred thousand volts," said Ryan. "Then it's bye bye."

Byte raised his tiny eyebrows.

"It means, 'I'm going away but I'll see you again soon,'" Peotry explained.

"I thought so," whispered Byte. "So, bye bye."

And he was gone.

"Oh!" Peotry cried.

They were all a little taken aback by Byte's sudden disappearance into the electric socket but Mr Willow said that he knew what he was doing, that he was an explorer.

"What's he going to explore in there?" Beth asked.

"The National Grid, I think," whispered Mr Willow, a little worried at the prospect, but not nearly as worried as he would have been if he knew what was about to happen.

A minute or so later, Mrs Willow called from the living room where she was watching her favourite soap opera.

"Darling, the television's on the blink."

"Oh, oh," whispered Mr Willow.

He went into the living room to see the television picture in all kinds of trouble, breaking up into lines and dots and emitting crackling noises. Then the living room light started to flicker. All the lights in the house flickered.

Once.

Twice.

Then they went out.

And the television went dead.

"Oh, oh," Mr Willow whispered again, a little louder this time.

"What's happening?" Peotry asked in the sudden darkness.

"Somebody get a torch!" Mr Willow called. "Darling, have we got any candles?"

"I think so," replied Mrs Willow, bumping into tables and chairs as she went to get them.

"I'll open the curtains," said Ryan. "We can get some light from outside."

He opened the curtains, just in time to see the most amazing sight.

"Wick...ed!" Ryan exclaimed.

"What is?" Beth asked.

She looked. They all looked.

Outside, street by street, block by block, mile by mile, the whole of the city was going black.

"I haven't heard of anything like this for years," said Mr Willow. "Power cuts, like in the 1970s."

Within a minute they were in total darkness, the kind of darkness that you never know in cities, a thick darkness in which you cannot even see your hand in front of your face.

"Daddy, I'm scared," said Peotry.

"Hold my hand," Ryan said. "If you can find it. There, you're alright now."

"This is Byte's doing," Mr Willow said in the darkness. "I know it! This is him!"

"Byte couldn't do all this," Beth said. "He's tiny!"

"He's special," said Mr Willow. "Believe me, this is Byte's doing."

"Daddy!" cried Peotry. "It's dark!"

"I've found matches," Mrs Willow called out. "Be careful everyone, I'm going to light one."

There was a scraping sound and suddenly a hole in the darkness appeared. Mrs Willow's face, or part of it, appeared in the faint yellow light, like a ghost.

"We've got candles somewhere," she said, looking around in the shadows.

Peotry heard her mother say something rude as the match went out.

"I still can't see!" cried Peotry.

"I've got you," said Ryan. "We're alright."

"Here," called Mrs Willow who had found a candle after the fourth match had gone out. "Be very careful. I'm going to put it in the centre of the table."

In a couple of minutes the living room was lit by a solitary candle and they could all see again. Just.

"Last one," said Mrs Willow. "There are such things as torches, you know, sweetheart. We should be prepared."

"Let's hope Byte finds what he's looking for soon," said Mr Willow, but he had his doubts, first that it would be soon, and second that Byte actually knew what he was looking for. It had sounded to Mr Willow that Byte was looking for something quite mysterious.

They wondered if they were all going to get arrested for bringing the city into darkness when they heard a new voice, but it wasn't Byte.

"It's my radio," said Beth.

Beth fiddled with the dials, tuning in until she got a clear reception.

"...into darkness. Please stay in your homes. Keep your radios tuned and listen. There is nothing to be alarmed about. Reliable sources tell us that the power loss is due to a massive electrical surge and is being attended to at this very moment. There is no danger and you are advised to stay in your homes. If you are using candles, please take extra special care. Use torches wherever possible..."

The broadcast went on but as yet they didn't know that the power cut had been caused by a miniature explorer about five millimetres high, and even if they'd known, they wouldn't have said so.

"Oh dear," said Mrs Willow. "I'll get William."

"I don't like it," Peotry cried.

"You're safe," said Ryan, lifting her up onto his lap, "I still can't believe Byte could do all this."

"I do," said Mr Willow. "I don't know how, but I'm sure it was him. I just hope he knows what he's doing."

"I don't think he does," said Beth. "He only knows The Inside, not The Outside. I mean, he thought the world was flat!"

"Well he's mucking up The Outside good and proper," said Mr Willow. "I wonder what rules he's following."

"Perhaps there are rules he doesn't know about," said Beth.

This was possible. Byte was an explorer from the quantum world and as an explorer there were many things he didn't know. It was very possible that he might cause great damage if he wasn't careful, and even if he was careful.

"Sssh!" said Mr Willow. "Listen!"

On the radio an agitated commentator's voice was saying,

"... from Hinkley Point B Nuclear Power Station news is coming in of a dangerous overload.."

Everyone gasped.

"And from Torness Nuclear Station a similar build up. News now from the coal-fired station at Fiddlers Ferry of a complete loss of power. And as I speak, news is

coming in from virtually all United Kingdom main and sub-stations of disruption to the National Grid and dangerous overloads..."

"Nuclear Stations!" repeated Ryan in horror.

"Is it bad news?" Beth asked.

"That's an understatement," said Mr Willow with a tight voice.

"Is it Byte's fault?" Peotry asked. "Is he being bad?"

"Doesn't matter much if his intentions are good or bad," said Mr Willow. "The thing is, he's getting us into a whole lot of trouble."

Ryan held Peotry's hand as they listened to the terrifying radio broadcasts.

"The nuclear power station at Dungeness is reporting extreme fluctuations. The nuclear plant at Hunterston is reporting similar problems. Problems from all major stations are still being reported. Every major city is in darkness. The whole of the United Kingdom is in darkness. The United States and NATO have gone to full alert in case of sabotage or terrorist attack."

"Good grief!" exclaimed Mr Willow. "United States! NATO! What is he doing?"

"He can't help it," pleaded Peotry. "He's just trying to learn."

"Couldn't he read a book," suggested Mrs Willow, cradling William. "It's much safer."

"He can't read," said Peotry.

"You should teach him," said Mr Willow. "If we're all still alive."

"Are we going to die?" Peotry asked. "Is Byte going to kill us all?"

"Of course not," said Mrs Willow. "Don't frighten the children, darling," she whispered to Mr Willow.

Gonka the cat trotted into the darkened room totally unperturbed and jumped onto Beth's lap where she purred away contentedly. Beth stroked her and listened to another announcement.

"Reports are coming in of more power failures across the country. Reactors at all nuclear stations are being carefully monitored..."

Ryan said something in a loud whisper, but no one heard what it was, fortunately.

The announcements went on, power failure after failure, warning after warning, for about an hour. The family sat in the dark, listening, wondering, hoping.

"Government spokesmen say there is nothing to be alarmed about..."

"And pigs might fly," said Mrs Willow.

"Sssh!"

"...There appears to be no threat from outside. This is purely a national problem. Experts have been called in to investigate the breakdown of the grid...."

"Nothing to be alarmed about?" Ryan said in amazement. "Every nuclear station in the country out of control, total darkness and nothing to be alarmed about? Do they think we're stupid?"

"Of course they do," said Mrs Willow. "They're politicians."

"Strange," said Mr Willow, "when I saw Byte this morning he looked so tiny and harmless, it didn't occur to me that by the end of the day he would have blown up the entire British Isles."

"He hasn't," said Mrs Willow. "He must know what he's doing."

"Hmm," said Mr Willow, doubtfully.

The Willows watched the candle burn down, listening to the radio and talking quietly to each other. It was unnerving, sitting in the gloom of their living room, the whole country in darkness, knowing that they alone knew the cause of this massive and frightening power failure.

"It could be a coincidence," suggested Mrs Willow. "It might not be Byte."

Mr Willow simply cleared his throat. This was Byte's doing, clear as daylight.

"Perhaps we should telephone the Prime Minister," Beth said.

"And say what?" Ryan asked. "'Hello, Prime Minister. This is The Willow family here. We know why the country is about to be blown up. You see, it's this little creature called Byte. He popped out of my sister's computer this morning and wants to find out about The Outside. He jumped into the National Grid and is looking for The Power. I'm terribly sorry. He doesn't mean any harm and I'm sure he won't be long.' What do you think the Prime Minister will say? 'Oh, I see! Well, thank you for telling us. Jolly good. Bye bye.'"

"I just thought," said Beth. "It doesn't seem right sitting here in the dark without telling anyone."

"Ryan's right," said Mr Willow. "No one would believe us."

So they sat talking, listening, waiting.

They lost track of time for quite a while, aware only that the candle was almost burnt out.

At last the announcer arrived with some better news saying that some stations were sending more positive reports. Nuclear power stations were stabilising. All indications were that the emergency might be nearing an end.

"Phew!" sighed Mr Willow.

"Come on, Peotry!" said Mrs Willow, still carrying William who was fast asleep. "Let's get you and your little brother to bed."

Peotry yawned and didn't object as she was very tired. It had been a long day with many strange things happening.

They put William into his cot, then Peotry felt her way into her own bedroom, undressed and climbed into bed, her mother helping her in the darkness.

"Is Byte alright?" Peotry asked. "Is he coming back?"

"Maybe," said Mrs Willow. "I don't understand him or what he is."

"Is the darkness really his fault, Mum?"

"Probably, Peotry, but I'm sure he doesn't mean it. I just hope he can put it all right."

"I think he will," said Peotry. "I know he will. He's good."

Hardly had Mrs Willow left the room when Peotry heard a familiar sound. Opening her eyes she saw Byte sitting by her computer.

"Hello, Peotry."

"Hello, Byte."

"I've had a bit of an adventure," said Byte.

"So have we," Peotry answered. "All the lights went out and the television stopped and the whole world was going to explode."

"Oh, dear," said Byte. "Did I do that? I'm sorry, Peotry. You see, I didn't know how

The Inside touches The Outside. But I'm learning. I'm certainly learning."

"That's good," said Peotry. "Does that mean England isn't going to blow up now?"

"I don't see why it should," said Byte. "I left everything as I found it. It's so very interesting. I wish you could come with me, I'd show you around."

"They were ever so worried," Peotry said. "Mum and Dad and Ryan and Beth. Everyone. We were all in the dark because there was a power cut. There were no lights anywhere. I was scared."

"I didn't mean to scare you, Peotry," said Byte, "but I was so fascinated. A whole new set of rules to learn."

"I think you must have broken lots of them," said Peotry, "to make so many things go wrong."

"I've come to a conclusion," said Byte. "I think that I've got something a bit different to my brothers and sisters."

"What's that?" Peotry asked.

"I didn't know what to call it at first," said Byte, "except it lets me choose what I want to do. It makes me, *me*. Do you know what I mean?"

Peotry said she didn't.

"You do," said Byte, "but you don't know you do. This thing makes me Byte and them," he said affectionately, pointing inside the computer, "*them*!"

"I don't understand," said Peotry. "Will you tell me in the morning?"

"Can't I tell you now?" Byte asked.

"I think I have to go to sleep," said Peotry dreamily. "Maybe this is all just a dream anyway."

"What's a dream?" Byte asked.

"You don't know anything, do you Byte?"

"I do," replied Byte, proudly. "I know a lot more than I did this morning. But the most important thing is what I have just learned. You see, Peotry, I always thought I had to follow the rules, but I just did something I shouldn't have been able to do. In fact, all day long, ever since I met you I've been doing things I shouldn't be able to do. That is what Human Errors would call exciting. I'm going to do what you are doing now,

Peotry. I'm going to lay down here and think about today. I wonder if my head is big enough to think about it all. Peotry? Peotry?"

Peotry was already fast asleep and Byte watched her for quite a long time thinking that he needed another new word to describe this first Human Error he'd met. Tomorrow he would find it. That was if The Willows were not too angry with him for what he'd done.

The Willows were, in fact, very relieved, for the lights had come back on in their home and everywhere, and the power stations were back to normal and England was not going to be blown up. They went to bed in good spirits but full of wonder at the amazing creature which had popped into their home, determined that first thing in the morning, should Byte still be around, they would have a talk with him to make sure he never did such a thing again.

Little did they know that just as they were planning to set this new rule for Byte, Byte was considering and marvelling at the sheer magic and delight of Free Will.

Bit 5: Action at a Distance

"So you see, Byte," said Mr Willow, "what you did was very dangerous."

Byte tried to look repentant, but he was still exhilarated by his adventures.

"You upset an enormous number of people. Millions of homes had no light, no heat, no food."

Byte had learned the rule that saying sorry was often useful, but like a lot of Human Error rules, didn't always work.

"No one knew what was happening. You very nearly caused a war."

Mr Willow was still upset, despite the apology.

When Byte looked mystified, he had to explain,

"A war, Byte is bad, very bad, in fact, the worst kind of bad you can imagine."

Byte had already picked up the notion that there was a great difference between good and bad, though he couldn't always tell them apart.

In the face of all these uncertainties, Mr Willow found it difficult to scold the tiny creature.

"Didn't you know what you were doing?" he asked, as mildly as possible.

"No," said Byte. "I got carried away."

They were in Mr Willow's car. It was Saturday morning, eight o'clock, and they were driving through the streets of London to the office where Mr Willow worked. Mr Willow had been reluctant to take Byte with him, especially now, knowing the damage Byte could do, but he had promised and he liked to keep promises. Ryan sat next to his father, holding the matchbox in which Byte sat, bobbing up and down with the movement of the car.

"You're in the north of London," said Ryan, "travelling at fifteen miles an hour in a car which can do one hundred and twenty miles an hour because it's stuck in a traffic jam."

"Can you lift me higher?" Byte asked.

Ryan lifted the matchbox up until Byte could see out of the car's side window. Byte's eyes opened wide and he dived down into the matchbox.

"It's quite safe," said Ryan.

Byte came out again, slowly, gripping the edge of the matchbox, staring at the streets.

"So wonderful!" he exclaimed. "So …big!"

There was a look of innocent wonder in Byte's face which made Ryan smile.

"You came close to blowing all this up, you know," said Ryan.

Byte knew. He would try not to do it again.

"What are all these buildings for?" he asked. "Do Human Errors live in them?"

"Some," said Ryan. "In others they just work."

Byte tried to distinguish between work and live, live and work. He asked Ryan to explain.

"Living," said Ryan, who didn't find it that easy, "is doing what you want. Work is doing what you have to do in order to do what you want."

Byte rolled Ryan's explanation around in his tiny head.

"Work is 'Do this, do that'?" he asked.

"Sort of," answered Ryan.

"Yesterday," Byte said, "I did what I wanted. I looked for The Power. Nothing told me to do it, I just did it. This was a truly wonderful thing. I chose to do something and I did it. This is called Free Will, is that right?"

"Yes," said Mr Willow, "but it isn't freedom to cause harm. You must be careful."

He was worried about two things; first, about the problem at work, which is why he had to go to his office on a Saturday morning; second, about Byte. Byte wanted to help but Mr Willow was afraid he might do more harm than good.

He glanced down at the tiny figure peering over the edge of a matchbox into The Outside World. He still felt that it might all be a dream and that he would wake up with everything back to normal, but there was nothing normal about chatting to a quantum creature who could blow up the entire Earth.

"I will try," said Byte, which was encouraging.

They arrived at the building where Mr Willow worked and parked the car. Ryan closed the matchbox as they went into the lift, up to the eleventh floor and into Mr Willow's office.

"Bad news Ryan, Draper's here."

Andrew Draper was Mr Willow's manager. They didn't like each other and when Ryan met Mr Draper he knew why. Draper was a burly man with a sour face and eyes like lasers.

"Willow," said Draper, "in on a Saturday, well, well, well. Worried, are you?"

"I want to sort the problem," said Mr Willow.

"Yours to sort," said Draper. "Who's this?"

"I'm..."

"Willow junior, I suppose," said Draper. "Need your son's help, do you Willow?"

"I thought I..." Ryan started.

"I'm closing the office at two o'clock," Draper said roughly. "If you can't sort it I'll find someone who can. No job is for life, you know."

Without waiting for an answer, Draper headed upstairs back into his office.

"Wow!" said Ryan. "He's worse than our headmaster."

"Isn't he just," agreed Mr Willow. "Come on. We'd better get started."

Mr Willow logged onto his computer while Ryan took Byte on a tour of the office. Byte had heard Mr Draper and begun to see the difference between one Human Error and another.

The main office was open with lots of desks and on most of them was a computer. Mr Willow had his own small area, Draper a grand space upstairs.

Ryan sat in a high-backed comfortable chair, feeling like a true executive.

"Nice," he said.

Byte wandered around a desk feeling the wood, the smoothness of plastic in the desk tidy, the softness of a mouse mat, the coldness of the telephone, the thinness of paper, the textures of pencils, pens, rulers, rubbers, sharpeners… everything.

"So many touches," he whispered.

He stopped at a calendar.

"What's this?" he asked.

Ryan tried to explain but Byte didn't understand days and nights and months and years and was amazed that Human Errors would want to count time this way.

"You must need a lot of paper," he said, "to count so many passing moments."

They joined Mr Willow who was staring at rows of figures with one hand on his forehead, looking distraught.

"There's something wrong," he said to Ryan. "These figures," he pointed to a part of the screen, "are too high and these are too low, but I don't know why. There are over a million customers," said Mr Willow, "thousands of companies and bank accounts, millions of transactions, cheques, cards, telephone orders. The mistake could be anywhere!"

"May I help?"

It was Byte, peeking over the side of the matchbox.

Mr Willow showed Byte the screen and Byte's eyes went up and down, left and right, trying to follow the movements of the numbers until he lost his balance and fell over.

"It is not my way of seeing," he said, brushing himself down in a very cute way. "I could look easier from the inside."

"Do you know what to look for?" Ryan asked.

"I will just look," answered Byte, "and see what I can find."

"Now be careful," warned Mr Willow. "No more blackouts."

"No problem," Byte answered, and disappeared.

"I wonder what scientists would make of Byte," sighed Mr Willow. "Oh, oh. Here we go again."

The computer data began to move faster until it turned into a green blur.

"God save England," whispered Mr Willow. "I wonder what he's doing?"

"What who's doing?" came a sharp voice.

Draper. He never knocked, just barged in.

"What's going on?" he asked.

"Nothing," said Mr Willow, "It's alright. It's..."

"Doesn't look alright to me," said Draper. "I hope your son hasn't wrecked it, Willow."

"He never..."

"Because if he has he can pay for it."

"I..." Ryan tried to speak.

"Switch it off," said Draper.

"It isn't necessary," said Mr Willow. "We...", but Draper leaned over and switched off the computer.

'Don't come out, Byte!' Ryan prayed.

"Why don't you just leave it and go home," Draper said. "You're useless, both of you. Two of a kind. I don't want all my computers broken."

"We'll stay a little while longer," Mr Willow said, quickly enough to finish the sentence without being interrupted. Draper muttered something then stomped off.

Mr Willow turned on the computer again and Byte popped out. He sat on the ENTER button and looked at father and son with a puzzled expression.

"Well?" asked Mr Willow.

"Difficult," said Byte. "I will have to do some deeper digging."

"Deeper digging? You mean Head Office?"

"Do I?"

"I don't know, but our information is in different countries. There are offices in Japan, Germany, the United States and Australia."

"Interesting," said Byte. "Can you come with me?"

"To all these countries?" exclaimed Mr Willow. "No, of course not."

"Can't you go on your wheels?" Byte asked.

"You mean the car?"

It was obvious Byte had no sense of distance or time in The Outside.

"That's not possible. These places are thousands of miles away. There are seas and oceans in between."

Byte sat very still, humming to himself, which was very cute.

"I will have to go alone," he said.

"Can you do that?" Mr Willow asked. "All the way to Europe, Japan, America and

Australia? Australia is the other side of the world!"

"From The Inside," said Byte, "it is all one."

"I'm not sure what that means," said Mr Willow, "but whatever you do, you have to be careful not to get The Inside into a mess. If The Inside is in a mess, The Outside is a worse mess."

"The Inside is never a mess," said Byte. "The Inside is always in order."

"Look," Mr Willow said, anxiously, "whatever you do, don't mess up, Byte."

"I'll try," said Byte, "but before I go, I want you to know that the man who was here..."

"Mr Draper?"

"Yes. He is joined to your computer. He knows what you are doing. He is watching you."

"Watching me?" Mr Willow asked. "Why would he want to do that?"

Byte shrugged.

"I found you in his computer. Shall I make him not see you?"

"Strange!" said Mr Willow. "Yes, please, do that."

"I will be a little longer this time," said Byte. "I have to do what your cleverer Human Errors call 'Action at a Distance'."

Mr Willow looked dubious.

"Well, if you must, but BE CAREFUL!"

Byte did his vanishing trick leaving Mr Willow and Ryan alone.

"Fancy Draper tapping into my computer," whispered Mr Willow.

"That's sneaky," said Ryan. "Perhaps there's something he doesn't want you to find out."

They watched the screen in silence for a moment, then the door suddenly burst open and Draper burst in again. He was furious.

"What's going on down here?" he shouted.

"Not a lot," replied Mr Willow. "Why?"

"Why? Because my computer's on the blink now, that's why. Nothing but funny little green men raining down from the sky."

Ryan smiled.

"Something funny, sonny Jim?" Draper asked Ryan.

"No," Ryan answered, "only..."

"Don't let him tamper with the computers," warned Draper. "These teenage kids think they have all the answers."

"I just..."

"If it's a virus," said Draper, "and your kid put it on, he pays to take it off."

"I don't think..."

"And if you don't sort things out by one o'clock, you're out."

"Out?"

"Out of a job, Willow! I'm fed up with your fluffing around. One o'clock!"

He left the room, banging the door shut behind him.

Father and son looked at each other, then sat and watched the screen.

And waited.

And waited.

The computer sparked into life and a message appeared on the screen with lots of strange symbols, then the line:

Please Enter your password.....

"Good heavens!" exclaimed Mr Willow. "That's our Head Office in Japan."

"Put in the password, Dad."

"I can't Ryan. I don't know it."

But no sooner had Mr Willow spoken than letters appeared on the monitor, one by one, replacing the dots on the line of the password. When it was entered, Mr Willow pressed the ENTER button.

Thank you.
The password is correct.
Please type in your security level.
.....

"Dad?"

"I'm Level Three," said Mr Willow. "Draper is two. One is the highest."

"Say one then," said Ryan.

Mr Willow typed '1' and a new message appeared.

Please enter your security code.

"I don't have one," said Mr Willow. "You don't need it at Level Three."

but the code filled itself in!

Thank you.
You have access at Security Level 1.
How can we help you?

"That's amazing!" exclaimed Ryan. "Byte's brilliant!"

Mr Willow typed away, finding out what he needed to know and printing out lots of figures.

"I feel like a thief," he said to Ryan. "A hacker."

"But you're not, Dad. Someone else is the thief, somewhere else, and you're going to find them out."

Mr Willow typed as fast as he could. For an hour he was madly busy while Ryan collected the printouts, labelled them and kept them tidy.

"My goodness!" Mr Willow whispered to himself.

"What's up?" Ryan asked.

"Wait," he replied. "I need to be sure about this."

Another half hour passed. Whenever special codes were needed, they filled themselves in until complicated lines of computer language appeared. Mr Willow was stumped.

"These bits are gobbledygook to me," he said.

"Not to me," said Ryan. "Let me see."

Ryan sat down. Some of the lines of code flashed on and off, perhaps to draw his attention.

"This is very clever…"

What they discovered was that someone was taking tiny amounts of money from millions of bank accounts, and millions of tiny amounts made one huge amount. But who was doing it?

"The company will be destroyed, thousands of people will lose their jobs and somebody somewhere – like me - is going to take the blame for it."

They worked together until, with endless help from Byte, they found the villain.

"Dad! It's him!"

There on the screen was the name 'Mr A. Draper' and alongside were other names, including,

"Archibald Pole! He's the one who sent you the letter, Dad! The father of that boy in Beth's class!"

Mr Willow wasn't sure whether he could believe what he saw.

"Dad. This is a conspiracy!"

"Yes it is, Ryan, but we're going to turn it around, aren't we? Can we do it? Can HE do it?" he said, meaning Byte.

He could. An alarm was triggered that sent messages to every office in every country. Mr Willow squeezed his son's shoulder. What a team!

> *Message to Mr Willow and Ryan.*
> *Back soon*
> *Byte*

"He's a little genius!" said Ryan.

"Yes he is, isn't he?" said Mr Willow and they both danced around the chairs until the door opened and Mr Draper burst in.

"What the devil are you two doing?" he bellowed. "Have you taken leave of your senses?"

"Yes, I think we have... Draper."

"*Mister* Draper to you, Willow. Who do you think you are?"

"We're the Willows," said Mr Willow. "Beware the Willows! The wind in the Willows will blow you away!"

"You're mad, you are, Willow. No wonder you're getting this company into trouble. You're fired, do you hear? Fired. Go home, now!" and he banged his way out and stomped his way up to his office.

At that very moment in Tokyo, some very clever people working through the night received an alarm on their computer. It told them who was tampering with the system and putting their company into trouble. They called their team leader who called his line manager who called the section leader who called the deputy manager who told the managing director who screamed down the telephone line to New Scotland Yard who screeched their way to Mr Andrew Draper's office who they promptly arrested, all within minutes.

Also at that moment, a very smart and wealthy microchip designer sitting in his home in Japan was in a state of shock because he had seen a tiny creature sitting on the F2 key of his computer keyboard.

"Not possible!" said the microchip designer to himself in Japanese, and indeed, when he looked again, the little creature had gone. But he was sweating and wondering whether to give up designing microchips and turn to something else for a living.

Mr Willow and Ryan watched the police arrive and take Draper away. One of the senior officers congratulated them and said they'd been magnificent IT detectives.

When Byte came back, he found Mr Willow and Ryan in excellent spirits.

"Did I help?" he asked, sliding down the plastic casing of the keyboard.

"Did you help!" repeated Mr Willow, exuberant. "You were... magnificent!"

"If it wasn't for you," said Ryan, "Dad might have ended up in prison, a place where Human Errors go when they really do make human errors. How did you do it, Byte? All those passwords and codes! Amazing! Beautiful!"

"'Beautiful. Beautiful'", repeated Byte. "That is a nice word. But these words and numbers weren't beautiful."

"They were to us," said Mr Willow, rather excited for a grown man. "And you did all this without getting the world into the same mess as last night!"

"I tried not to upset the balance," said Byte, thoughtfully, "though there was a little quantum uncertainty in Tokyo."

"Whatever that means!" said Mr Willow. "I'm so relieved! Let's go home."

So it was only in the car radio that they heard the news that over a hundred thousand computers in the centre of Tokyo had all suddenly been affected by a virus that sent little smiling faces raining down the screens.

"Oops," whispered Mr Willow.

Byte was staring out of the car window again, thinking his own mysterious thoughts.

"It won't do any harm," said Byte, "just to say 'Hello'."

Mr Willow shook his head. He looked at Ryan who looked back at him. Then they both looked at Byte.

He was staring through the car window at The Outside, as innocent as a new born baby.

they both danced around the chairs

Bit 6: Bonanza

The Bonanza Supermarket was not so much a large shop as a small town. Mrs Willow remembered shopping when she was a girl. You could have a chat, she recalled, with the grocer or the baker or the chemist. You could walk to the shops and back without having to take a car, get stuck in traffic, queue to get in, queue to get out and feel in the end as if you'd been on a day trip to Greedygrubland and back.

These thoughts were in her mind as she drove into the Bonanza Car Park with its Welcome signs and painted arrows that led her through the usual maze of cars to a rare empty space.

It was very busy.

Especially on a Saturday afternoon.

Mrs Willow hadn't got used to the sheer numbers of people, like bees around a hive, only it wasn't a hive. It was a supermarket. Or rather, a hypermarket. Or perhaps a superhypermarket. 'How big is big?' thought Mrs Willow.

Well, Bonanza was the biggest.

Thirty-five checkouts.

Cash tills that looked as if they had been taken from a spaceship.

And food, food, food.

So much of it from every corner of the world, all neatly wrapped and packaged and ready to be eaten.

"What's the matter, Mum?" Peotry asked. "You've gone all quiet."

"I was thinking," said Mrs Willow, "how different this all was when I was a girl."

Byte was sitting in his matchbox on Peotry's lap and holding out the palm of his hand as Ryan had shown him. Peotry touched the tiny hand lightly with her little finger which seemed enormous in comparison.

"What is this place?" he asked as Peotry lifted the matchbox up to the level of the window.

"It's a supermarket," said Beth. "We buy food here."

Peotry pointed into her mouth and rubbed her tummy.

"Human Errors have to eat," explained Mrs Willow. "I just wonder if we have to eat so much," she said looking at the truly vast Bonanza.

"I would like to be able to eat too," said Byte, "but I'm not sure what will happen to my insides."

"Come on," Mrs Willow said. "Let's get going."

Byte hid inside Peotry's Mickey Mouse watch, staring at Peotry.

"Look, Mum!" Peotry cried with delight.

They left their car and headed for the Bonanza, Peotry feeling proud and important that she had Byte with her, and that no one else on Earth had anything like him.

"This is the way in," said Peotry. "These are the fruits and vegetables, these are oranges, these are apples, pears, grapes, plums, lemons, bananas..."

"Don't tell him everything," said Beth. "He'll never remember."

Byte's eyes rolled around, taking in the beautiful colours.

Peotry was so attentive to Byte that she didn't notice a small boy staring at her until he tapped her on the shoulder and said,

"Who are you talking to?"

"No one," said Beth, giving the boy a 'Get Lost' look.

"I saw her talk to the watch," insisted the boy, "and the watch talked back. Daddy," he called to his father and tugged his sleeve, "I saw her watch talk. Its eyes moved."

The father looked around and said to Mrs Willow,

"I'm sorry. He's a good boy, usually."

"That's alright," laughed Mrs Willow, a little nervously.

"Always making up stories, aren't you Joey?" said the father.

Joey shook his head to say no, his eyes fixed on Peotry's watch which, with a sudden, sharp movement he tried to grab. Peotry jerked her arm out of the way and slapped Joey on his hand.

"Serves you right," said Joey's father. "Sorry, young lady," he said to Peotry, and pulled Joey away.

"Nosey Parker!" Beth muttered, and Peotry stuck her tongue out at Joey.

Beth pushed the trolley feeling very grown up whilst Mrs Willow kept checking her shopping list and piling up a small mountain of food.

"This is milk," explained Peotry to the wide-eyed Byte, "and cheese and butter and margarine and ..."

"He'll never remember," said Beth again.

But Byte was remembering everything, staring from the watch face at endless vistas of food all destined to be dropped into the insides of Human Errors, so much so that he wondered why Human Errors didn't burst apart.

"These are tins," said Peotry, "soup, beans, peas, tomatoes, potatoes..."

"Oh stop it!" said Beth. "You're being boring."

"I'm not," Peotry said. "Byte wants to learn and I'm teaching him."

She carried on down the next aisle.

"Biscuits," she said, "chocolaty, gingery, fruity, nutty, all kinds. I like these," and she took down a packet of wafers. Being small, she had to reach up and stretch out the hand with the watch. Byte couldn't resist the temptation. He'd had an idea and wanted to see if it worked.

He jumped from the watch out onto the wafers, just as Peotry lost her balance and knocked them all over.

"Peotry!" cried Mrs Willow, exasperated.

"Beth!" Peotry whispered to her sister. "Byte's out!"

Beth checked the Mickey Mouse watch and looked at Peotry with her eyes wide open and her hand over her mouth.

"I saw!"

They turned to see Joey and his father. Joey was looking at Peotry with a wicked expression, but his father wanted to help.

"Let me," Joey's father said, starting to pack the wafers up again. Beth and Peotry looked at each other and kept their fingers crossed.

It didn't work.

All of a sudden Joey's father stopped dead.

"What's the matter?" Joey asked.

"I thought I saw... I thought... I saw..."

Peotry and Beth both gulped.

Mrs Willow looked at her two daughters, then at Joey and his father, and groaned.

"It's alright!" she said, quickly. "We'll put them back."

"I must be seeing things," said Joey's father. "I thought I saw... but no... that's impossible... Good grief, there it is again!"

Sure enough, there was Byte, running up the biscuits to the very top.

"I told you!" said Joey. "It was in her watch."

"What on Earth is it?" Joey's father asked.

"Nothing," said Mrs Willow.

She tried to grab Byte but he'd reached the top of the shelves and ducked into an electric strip light.

"Oh no!" whispered Peotry.

"Drat!" cried Beth.

"Bother," said Mrs Willow.

"Good grief!" said Joey's father again.

Joey just stared up, too small to see what had happened. Some other shoppers, seeing the small group staring up at the shelves also stopped and stared, even though there was nothing to see. Soon, a little crowd had gathered.

"What is it?" someone asked.

"It's a little man," Joey called out.

"A little man? Where?" someone called out.

"He belongs to that girl there," Joey pointed. "He came out of her watch and ran up the biscuits."

"Rubbish! What are we standing here for like idiots!"

"It's true, isn't it?"

Joey's father was already beginning to doubt what he had seen and half nodded, half shook his head.

The manager of the Bonanza came along to see what all the fuss was about.

"It's a little man," laughed one watcher. "Kid says he saw a little man. And his father said so, too."

"A little man?" the manager repeated, and then, quite sensibly, "How little?"

"Very little," said Joey. "Littler than my little finger."

The manager looked up then turned to the crowd.

"I think it best if we all moved on," he said. "Just a silly joke. Best to keep moving. We're blocking the aisles. Please."

The crowd began to disperse when a voice called out, "There he is! There he is!"

Everyone was looking at the Bonanza digital clock high up on the wall at the front of the store. Instead of revealing the time, the clock showed a smiling face and robotically waving arm.

"That's him! That's him!" cried Joey.

"Good Lord!" exclaimed Joey's father.

The Bonanza manager immediately began to worry, mainly about his job. He had visions of his supervisors telling him off. 'Why did you let this happen?' they would ask. 'You're supposed to be running a smooth, efficient business, not a circus.' The manager felt very uncomfortable. This was not something he could easily explain away. Then, in a moment of inspiration, he said, albeit in a voice that was too bright and breezy,

"Ladies and gentlemen. It's just a message from the management, welcoming you to Bonanza."

The crowd seemed ready to accept this, but Joey called out,

"It's not true! It's a little man. He's real. We saw him!"

The manager would have liked to take Joey and do something nasty to him, but instead he just smiled and asked the crowd to disperse.

Then another shopper called out,

"If it's yours, mate, why's it saying that?"

Hello Peotry Willow.
Hello Beth Willow,
Hello Mrs Willow!

Peotry and Beth were delighted, but Mrs Willow wanted to sink into the floor and disappear.

The growing crowd wanted to know who were The Willows.

"They are!" shouted Joey, pointing to Peotry and her family. "It's their little man."

The manager went over to Mrs Willow and whispered quietly in her ear,

"Do you know anything about this?"

Mrs Willow did not know how to answer. If she said 'yes' she might get them all into trouble; if she said 'no' she would be lying.

"Me?"

"Yes. Do you?"

"Know anything about this?" she said, pointing to the clock.

"Yes."

"Do you think we did it?"

"Did you?"

A scream came from the adjacent aisle. The manager hurried around, closely followed by the crowd, to find one of his staff flat on the floor in a dead faint. Shoppers had gathered around to help.

"What's the matter, Maud?" the manager said. "What happened?"

"I... I... I..." stumbled Maud.

"You what?"

"I... I... I...saw a... oh!"

"Come on Maud," the manager said. "You're safe now. What did you see?" although he'd half guessed the answer already.

"Mr Price," which was a great name for a superdupermarket manager, "you'll never believe me."

"Try me, Maud."

"It was a little... a little..."

"Man?" suggested the manager.

Maud nodded.

"Where?" asked the manager.

Maud pointed to the lighting strips above the deep freeze.

"He was running along," she said. "He looked at me and waved, Mr Price. He waved. Just like this," and Maud waved at Mr Price who helped her to her feet, ordering some assistants to take her away for a glass of water and a rest.

The Willows had not followed the crowd.

"What are we going to do?" Mrs Willow whispered.

"We can't leave him," said Peotry. "We have to get him back."

"How?" Beth asked. "He makes greased lightning look slow."

"He doesn't mean to be bad, Mum. He's just curious."

"Whatever he is," said Mrs Willow, "and whatever he means to be, he's getting us into trouble and I don't like trouble. Let's go to the checkout and go home. Now!"

"But we can't leave him," pleaded Peotry. "It's not fair. He's all alone."

"He can look after himself," said Mrs Willow. "He's a clever little thing. You'll see, he'll turn up."

"He won't," Peotry said. "They'll catch him and squash him or put him in a little prison. They won't understand."

"Understand what, Peotry?" Mrs Willow asked.

"Him. They won't understand him!" cried Peotry, "and he won't understand them. He'll think we've left him and he'll blame us."

"Peotry's right, Mum," said Beth. "We can't just leave him."

"Well how are we supposed to find him?"

While the Willows were discussing how to find their lost Byte, rumours were spreading through Bonanza that something odd was afoot. The general feeling was that a creature was on the loose, small, maybe, but probably poisonous and dangerous.

"Ladies and gentlemen," the manager said over the growing babble of concern, "there's nothing to be alarmed about. Nothing."

"Then why all the screaming?" asked a burly man who liked a rumpus.

"She's a little nervous, that's all. She thought she saw something but it was nothing."

"We all saw something, too," said the burly man.

"I saw it," said the insistent Joey. "I did! I did!"

"What was it like, son?" asked the burly man.

"It was tiny," replied Joey, "and very quick. It looked like the man in the clock."

But the clock was just a clock again.

"You see," said the manager, "everything's back to normal."

"What's that, then?" asked a lady, staring at one of the Bonanza ceiling lights.

The lights of Bonanza were long tubes which ran along the length of each aisle from the entrance to the back wall. As they watched, they saw a shadowy spot whizzing along each tube in turn, down, up, down, up, leaving a tiny jet stream as it passed.

"It's only a moth," said a little old lady. "What do you want to go and make such a fuss about a moth for?"

"That's no moth," said the burly man. "Moths don't fly like that. Look at it. Straight as an arrow."

The line of flight was like a laser beam. People's heads turned as they followed the strange phenomena, as if they were at a tennis match.

Then the Bonanza lights started to flicker and spark.

"What's happening, Mum?" Peotry asked.

"I don't know Peotry, but I wish it wasn't."

The sparks were white at first, but soon changed to a whole rainbow of colours, dazzlingly bright and beautiful.

"Mummy!" exclaimed Beth. "Look at what he's done!"

Shoppers stopped and stared in wonder at the Bonanza Aurora Borealis.

"Amazing," somebody said.

"What a good idea!" said another.

"I hope it's not dangerous," said someone else.

"Turn the lights off!" ordered the manager. "Turn them off or there'll be a fire!"

Byte had simply wanted to please the Human Errors. He thought that despite the mountains of food, they looked sad and he was trying to make them happy.

When the lights were turned off there was an audible sigh of disappointment.

But it didn't last long.

A commotion was growing around one of the checkouts.

"I don't care if it's right or wrong," a customer was saying, a severe looking man with silver hair. "That's the total, that's what I'm paying!"

"But it's wrong," insisted the cashier with a puzzled look on her face. "It's wrong!"

"I can't stand here all day and wait for you to get the cost right," said the silver haired man. "Here's my money."

"I'm sorry, sir," said the cashier, "I'll have to call the manager. I won't keep you long," and she rang for Mr Price who was just beginning to relax after the excitement of the lights.

"What's the problem?" he asked the cashier.

"Nothing's wrong," interrupted the bad tempered man with silver hair, "except my time's being wasted waiting for this infernal machine to add up my money correctly."

"Yes, sir. Just a moment," said the manager quietly. "What's the problem, Martha?"

Martha, the cashier, said,

"It's not the gentleman's fault, but he's bought all this food," and she pointed to his full trolley, "and it adds up to three pounds and fifty-two pence."

"The total?" Mr Price asked.

"Yes, sir. The total. Three pounds and fifty-two pence."

Mr Price pressed a few buttons but the total would not change. People in the queue behind began to get edgy, as they do in supermarket lines if you are too slow. Mr Price said,

"I'm sorry, ladies and gentlemen, you'll have to move to another checkout. This one's faulty. I'm very sorry."

There were scowls and moans and insults, but people shuffled off to other queues.

"I'm sorry sir," said Mr Price turning to the silver haired man. "We'll have to recheck all your food."

"Nonsense," said the silver haired man. "She's already done it twice. That's the total, that's what I'll pay. You can't change the price now."

"I'm not changing the price," said the manager. "The till is wrong. It's not giving the correct figure."

He took a stuffed chicken and ran it through the bar code reader. Twelve pence appeared on the till display.

"Nothing wrong with that," said the silver haired man who had great presence of mind, a lot of nerve and was exceptionally greedy.

"I'm afraid there is," said the manager. "We'll have to take everything out and add it up by hand, otherwise you'll have to go through another checkout."

"You must be joking!" objected the silver haired shopper.

"Sorry, sir," insisted the manager, who was by now wishing himself home, away, or anywhere except where he was.

Then he had another idea.

"I'll tell you what sir," he said. "You leave me your name and address and I'll get the food delivered to you later on today. Free of charge. You just pay the correct amount on delivery."

The silver haired man started grumbling, unwilling to let things slip.

At that moment, more disturbances arose at other tills and the manager's heart sank as he heard scraps of conversation.

"Ten pence for a bottle of wine! Is it a sale?"

"Eleven pence for a basket of fruit! What a bargain!"

"Two pence for a yummy cake! Wow!"

"This is a real bonanza!" someone smirked.

Bells started to ring and lights flashed as the cashiers called for help. Each of them reported sales of goods at ridiculously low prices. Many of the assistants were trying to hold back customers who, seeing the main chance, were trying to persuade their cashiers to accept the unacceptable. People in the lines, pound signs spinning in their eyes, joined in the grumbles, pressurizing the cashiers to let them through and pay the silly amounts displayed on the till. The cashiers were doing their best, but beginning to panic as the news spread and the queues became longer and more agitated.

The manager made a short speech over the loudspeaker system.

"Ladies and gentlemen. We apologise for the problems at the checkouts. Something is wrong with the computer that controls the prices. Please be patient. The cashiers will have to add up your shopping for you by hand."

This didn't work for two reasons, first because the sums were too hard and secondly because most of the packages just had bar codes on them, not prices.

"You see how much we rely on technology," said a bright young man to the girl behind him. "When it goes wrong, we're sunk."

"I bet," said the girl, "that they can't even add up the prices on paper. It's too difficult for them."

But the two of them kept talking and arranged a date for later in the day, so something good came out of the disaster.

All this while, the Willows had been searching the Bonanza for Byte.

"It's worse than looking for a needle in a haystack," said Mrs Willow. "We'll never find him."

By now, the queues were long and very noisy.

"Oh dear," said Mrs Willow. "He's such a mixture of good and bad, isn't he?"

"He's not bad," Peotry said, and then with surprising wisdom added, "He just doesn't know how The Outside joins The Inside."

"Yes he does," Beth said. "I bet he's doing this because mum said food costs too much money."

"You mean he's doing this on purpose?" asked Mrs Willow. "Oh my! There'll be a riot," she warned. "I can see it coming!"

The queues were lengthening and becoming angrier by the moment, especially when people began to see one or two customers getting away with trolleys full of food at virtually no cost. One was the silver haired man who slipped out quietly, leaving a five pound note on the cash desk and telling the cashier to keep the change.

The manager told his staff to barricade the doors.

"What, fight the customers!"

"I don't know," replied Mr Price, desperately. "We can't let them go with all our food for nothing."

The staff had visions of fists flying at the doors of Bonanza, like a wild west fight at a saloon. Then the manager had yet another idea. It didn't matter that so far none of his ideas had worked, at least he kept having them.

"Ladies and gentlemen," he said over the radio, "once again I'm very sorry. What we have decided to do is charge you a flat rate to the nearest five pounds. We'll have to do some inspired guesswork, but we won't be far out. It's not ideal but it will get us out of this jam. Thank you."

It didn't work.

It could have done, but it didn't.

By now, all the customers saw pounds turning to pennies in front of them. They had all been taught to be oh so wary of spending their hard-earned money and to be exact. Exact. No flat rates where they might pay more than they owed. Exact. To the penny.

There was a mob spirit growing.

Individuals who were normally shy, perhaps a little scared and lonely, started gaining strength from each other and daring the un-dareable. All they needed was a leader.

"I've been here forty minutes!" shouted an angry young man. "I've had enough!" and he did what others had been thinking about. He rushed his trolley through the checkout and along to the exit.

Bells rang and staff converged to stop him, but other customers were following. They had waited and waited. All their lives they had waited for a moment to beat the system.

And this was it!

All the scruples and rules and fears and frights left them and they became, just for a few moments, rebels. Savages. Criminals.

Men and women, young and old, all turned to law breakers and ran. Even people who thought themselves fully in control of their actions found themselves running with their baskets and trolleys full of food.

The manager pressed an alarm and within a minute a police car howled up to the Bonanza with four tough looking policemen inside.

But what could they do against a stampede of angry, determined, desperate Bonanza customers, all obsessed with the same thought that for once in their lives they would get something for nothing.

The manager could only watch in disbelief as customers vaulted the checkouts and barged their way out into the car park beyond, each of them with a mad look in their eyes.

"This is wrong!" he called out over the loud speaker. "Please go back. Do not push. Please wait. Please go back!"

But they pushed on passed him. Lawyers, teachers, doctors, builders, plumbers, accountants, computer bods, taxi drivers, decorators, vets, journalists, scientists, street-cleaners, gardeners, bricklayers, roofers, writers, philosophers, even preachers, shopkeepers, butchers, bakers, candlestick makers, all, flew out through the door, eyes fixed and glazed, blaming everyone else, never themselves.

Bit 7: True Wisdom

"Did I do wrong again?" Byte asked.

He'd found his own way back to Peotry's watch. They hadn't run like everybody else, but the manager had let them go, too distraught to ask for their money. Now, a few hours later, Peotry was alone in her bedroom with Byte, talking about what had happened.

Peotry nodded.

Byte sighed and said, "I thought I was helping."

"I know that," said Peotry, "and Beth does, and probably mum does too, but she hates fusses and this was a big one."

"Why did things go wrong, Peotry?" Byte asked. "All I did was to make the food less money. I thought that was what Mrs Willow wanted."

"She did, but not like that," answered Peotry.

"When I saw them all running with their food," said Byte, "I thought I had done well and they were happy."

"They were running because they were scared," said Peotry. "If they were caught they might have had to go to prison. And the shop was angry because they lost all their money."

"Your rules are complicated," said Byte. "If I were you, I would make them simple."

"I can't do anything," said Peotry. "I'm only six."

Peotry had grown very fond of Byte. He was small, but he was cuddly. He felt like the best friend she had ever had and ever would have, someone who needed her and listened to her and treated her kindly. She didn't want him to leave.

"I have to go back soon, Peotry. I don't belong here and I can feel The Inside calling me. Perhaps they miss me after all."

"I'm sure they do. I'll miss you if you go."

Byte looked up at his new friend with his deep sparkling eyes and blinked.

"I have learned such a lot," he said, "and seen such a lot."

"Only a teeny bit of it," said Peotry. "There's much more. You'd have to spend years and years here and still you wouldn't see it all."

"I know," said Byte, "but I have to get back. They really do need me, you see, to keep the balance. It's a delicate thing, keeping the balance, but it has to be done; it's a rule. And don't forget, you're small too, for a Human Error, and there are billions of other Human Errors in the world, but they still need you."

They were silent for a few seconds, Inside and Outside having their own private thoughts.

"I would like you to do one more thing before I leave," said Byte. "Would you read me another story?"

"Course I will!" said Peotry, and decided on Rumpelstiltskin.

"Is that a good one?" Byte asked.

"It's a very good one. You sit down and get comfortable, then I'll begin."

Byte sat back in his daffodil and waited for his friend Peotry. He listened to the story intently, believing it all and wondering at it all, just as he had with all the stories she had read to him.

When it was over he looked anxious.

"Poor Rumpelstiltskin," he sighed.

"No!" said Peotry. "Poor Princess. Rumpelstiltskin was horrid."

"Horrid?" said Byte, "just because the princess couldn't change one thing to another?"

"That wasn't her fault," Peotry said. "Human Errors can't do that kind of thing."

"You can't?" Byte said, even more surprised. "There are so many things you can't do."

"Rumpelstiltskin was wicked," said Peotry. "He wanted to take away her baby."

"But she said he could," Byte reminded her.

"She had to," Peotry explained. "She didn't want him to. She had to!"

"But she could have another one," said Byte.

"Oh, Byte!" exclaimed Peotry. "Haven't you learned anything?" Byte wondered if he had. There was a lot to take in. He had obviously missed an important point. "Don't you have babies?" Peotry asked him.

Byte shook his head.

"That's terrible!" said Peotry. "Weren't you a baby once?"

"I am Byte," said Byte, "always have been, always will be."

Peotry told him that taking away a baby from its mother or father was the worst thing in the entire world.

"The worst?"

"Oh yes, the very worst. Rumpelstiltskin was wicked to do that. He deserved to be punished."

Byte thought hard.

"If I stayed here long," he said, "my spin would be unbalanced. There are so many things that mean everything to you and nothing to me."

"That's sad," said Peotry, wondering what Byte's 'spin' looked like.

"Sad for me," said Byte. "I wish I could be a Human Error for a minute, just to know what it must be like."

"Can't you be one?" Peotry asked. "If you can change things, can't you change yourself?"

"No," said Byte, "not that kind of change. I can move things around, but I can't change myself. That's against the rules."

"That's a shame," said Peotry. "It would be funny to see you big like me."

She laughed, and Byte laughed, the very first laugh he had made on The Outside, and it felt good. It was a Happy Moment.

"Could you do what Rumpelstiltskin did," Peotry asked, "and change straw to gold?"

"I don't know straw and I don't know gold," said Byte. "If I saw them and knew their insides I could change them, but it takes a lot of rearranging."

Peotry showed him the pictures in her story book, pointing to straw and to gold. Byte studied them hard.

"Yes," he said. "Lots of work. They're very different. Have you got any straw?" Byte asked. "I'll try."

Before she could answer, and the answer would almost certainly have been no, there was a knock on the door and the rest of the Willow family looked in, Mr Willow holding William, Beth holding Gonka, Mrs Willow and Ryan.

"Can we come in?" Beth asked.

"We thought you might be upset," Mr Willow said to both of them.

"And we came to tell you not to worry," said Mrs Willow.

"Byte thinks you're angry with him, Mum," said Peotry.

"Not really," she said. "I know it wasn't his fault. He was just trying to learn."

"I told him how greedy people are," said Peotry. "He understands now."

"Been reading more stories to him, Peotry?" Mr Willow asked.

Peotry said that she'd been reading Byte the story of Rumpelstiltskin and he wanted to try to turn straw into gold too. It was just about understandable this strange quantum creature wrecking the National Grid, but turning straw to gold was magic, not physics.

"Does it have to be straw?" Ryan asked. "How about lead? Change lead to gold, Byte, that would be something."

Lead was a common metal whilst gold was the most precious. Throughout history people had dreamed of changing lead to gold, it was what the Philosopher's Stone was all about. It had once been the ultimate knowledge, the meaning of True Wisdom, but no one had ever done it. Ryan and his parents knew this whilst Beth and Peotry had heard something about the Philosopher's Stone through a story more famous than Rumpelstiltskin, and even this one, would ever be.

"Can I see some lead?" Byte asked.

Mr Willow disappeared into his bedroom for a few moments, returning with a small but heavy looking grey block about the size of Peotry's hand.

"Here," said Mr Willow, "it belonged to my grandfather. He was a jeweller and he used it in his work. I don't know exactly what for, but we've kept it all these years as a memento. It's solid lead. You're not saying you can change it into gold, are you?" he asked Byte.

"You couldn't do that. It's impossible," said Beth.

Byte studied it.

"Hard," he said. "Very hard."

"People have been trying for centuries," said Mr Willow. "Never been done. Probably can't be done. They thought that if they could do this, they would have mastered Nature, that they would know all there is to know. An old Theory of Everything. Just goes to show."

This interested Byte. He had never tried such a thing but he imagined it could be done, though he would have to be fast and strong. And to know everything would be just what he wanted, the very reason he came to The Outside. He had already seen an amazing amount and was beginning to wonder whether The Inside and The Outside were the whole story or whether there might be other sides, hidden away. He was dizzy with knowledge and hungry for more. This could be the key.

"Well, Byte?" Ryan asked. "Is it too difficult?"

"I'm not sure," Byte answered. "Many atoms, much work. Hard," he repeated. "Very hard."

"Ah, well..." Mr Willow began to say, knowing it was impossible, but then Byte said,

"I think I'll try it anyway. If I went back with True Wisdom, that would be something, wouldn't it?"

It would, although they were all pretty sure Byte couldn't do it.

"Do you need anything?" Ryan asked.

"Stamina," said Byte. "This will be tricky."

Byte had never done such a thing before, but he thought it possible. If he could agitate his brothers and sisters enough on The Inside, there were no rules to say he couldn't. And this was precisely the reason he had broken free in the first place, to learn.

"This might take a little time," he said. "Be patient with Byte."

"We will," they said.

And he was gone.

"I wish I knew how he did that," said Ryan.

They watched in silence for a minute or two, but nothing happened.

"Perhaps it's too hard for him," said Beth.

"Byte can do anything," replied Peotry, faithful as ever.

"Patience," Mrs Willow reminded them.

"Should have asked him what that means," Ryan said. "If Byte doesn't understand time he might mean an hour, a day even, perhaps a month."

"A year," suggested Beth.

"A century," said Mr Willow.

"A millennium," laughed Ryan. "Can't hang around forever, though, can we?"

They waited fifteen minutes but nothing happened. Mr Willow wandered away.

They waited another fifteen minutes and Mrs Willow left them.

"How come it's so slow?" Beth asked. "I mean he whizzes through computers and countries without any trouble."

"There's a lot of changing to do," Ryan said. "If it was easy we'd have found out how to do it ages ago. There are billions of atoms in there."

"I know he can do it," Peotry said.

"That's why Byte likes you," said Beth. "You believe in him."

"I do," said Peotry.

They waited a while longer, then Ryan disappeared. Beth and Peotry were left alone.

"By the time he comes out," said Beth, "our great, great, great, great, great, great, great, great, grandchildren will be sitting here watching and waiting."

She and Peotry laughed, then Beth left and Peotry was alone. She wondered if she would ever see Byte again. Computers were one thing but a lump of lead was another. He was an explorer and sometimes terrible things happened to explorers. She worried about him, lost inside something he didn't understand and not able to get out again.

A day passed, a whole day, and still no sign of Byte. The Willows looked in every now and again but the lead remained stubbornly grey. Peotry was reluctant to leave the room, but of course she had to. The others lost faith, but she never did. She kept thinking about Byte and hoping he was alright, even if he couldn't do this wonderful trick. It didn't matter. What she wanted was to see him again and to make sure they were still friends. She couldn't imagine going her whole life without seeing him one more time.

Another day passed. The Willows gathered together in Peotry's room every now and again to study the lead.

"True Wisdom evidently takes a while," sighed Mr Willow.

Every day they gathered together. It became a talking point and a habit, but they didn't really believe anymore.

Except Peotry. She couldn't accept that Byte was gone for good. He would never leave her without saying goodbye.

Two weeks passed. Two whole weeks of seven days with twenty fours in each day and three thousand six hundred seconds in each hour. Then double that. A whole month of waiting. The whole thing was fast becoming a memory.

"Time for bed, Peotry," said Mrs Willow at the end of another day. "I'm sure it was just too difficult for him. It's a pity, but there you are, all part of growing up."

They left her alone. but Peotry wasn't tired. She lay on her bed staring at the lead weight, trying to see Byte turning atoms of lead into atoms of gold. Her thoughts roamed here and there, but they never lost their centre, which was her little friend.

She had no idea how long she had been lying there when something caught her eye.

At first she thought it was a dream, but it wasn't.

"Mum! Dad! Beth! Ryan! Everyone! Look!"

She was up and out of bed, standing at the door, shouting at the top of her voice. Her family, rubbing their eyes, came racing out of their rooms to see what was wrong.

Nothing was wrong.

"There!" Peotry pointed.

Sure enough, a spot of gold had appeared on the outside of the lead weight.

"Well, I'll be…!" exclaimed Mrs Willow.

The spot was unmistakeably gold, and as they watched, it grew.

Slowly.

Very slowly.

Very evenly.

Byte The Computer Mite

"Oh, it's beautiful!" exclaimed Peotry. "I told you he could do it!"

it takes a lot of rearranging and a lot of energy

The others were silent as they watched the pure, shining gold replace the dull, grey lead, growing like a living thing.

"Good heavens!" Mr Willow said to himself.

"Wow!" Ryan whispered.

"Oh!" Beth said.

A quarter of the lead had turned to gold.

A half.

Three quarters.

The final quarter slowly turned from grey to gold until there was the smallest of dark spots left, just as a few minutes before there had only been the smallest of gold spots in a lead block.

And then, at last, it was done.

In front of the amazed Willow family was an ingot of pure, shining gold.

And Byte!

They stared at him in absolute disbelief, except Peotry who clapped her hands and almost cried with delight and relief.

"Phew!" he said. "Hard work! I'm beat!"

"I'm sure you are!" laughed Mrs Willow.

Byte looked pleased, but also tired. He had never worked so hard, but for all his hard work he didn't think he had found True Wisdom. Another Human Error, he had decided. They seemed to have so many wishy-washy ideas, these giants who lived on The Outside. So much they did was uncertain and, well, wrong. They had rules they didn't follow which weren't real rules at all, just ways of doing things. His rules were simple and there was never, ever any denying them.

The gold ingot was passed around the astonished family.

"We could sell it," Ryan said. "It must be worth pots of money."

"No!" said Peotry. "Never!"

"Peotry's right," said Mr Willow. "It wouldn't be right."

"We have to keep it forever," said Peotry, "to remember Byte."

This was true. Money was important, and the Willows needed it as much as anyone else to live, but it wasn't everything and they doubted whether selling it would make them happy, not for any money under the sun.

They stared at the transformed block and it seemed to stare back at them, evidence of something quite wonderful.

"Well," said Byte. "I really do have to go now. Do this, do that," he said ruefully, "but I will come back," he added, "one day."

"True alchemy at last!" exclaimed Mr Willow. "Well done Byte!"

"But not True Wisdom," said Byte, sadly. "Never mind, perhaps next time. Lift me up, Peotry," he said, "onto your computer."

Peotry lifted him and put him on the space bar.

"I will return," Byte said. "I promise."

"You'll forget us," she said.

"I won't forget you Peotry," said Byte.

Peotry wanted to hug Byte, he was so cute and so loving in his own tiny way.

They had all been touched by him. His innocence moved them and they didn't want to lose him. His voice had a sad edge to it and Peotry saw that his eyes were moist.

"I am leaking water again," said Byte. "I will die."

"You won't die," said Peotry. "You're just crying. You must be upset."

"Am I? My spin is a little strange," he replied. "Well, goodbye."

And he was gone.

Silence.

"That was a bit sudden," said Ryan.

"He doesn't understand," said Peotry.

"Understand what?" Ryan asked.

"How to be a Human Error," said Peotry.

"Poor thing," said Mrs Willow. "Can't feel, can't love, must be awful, even if he can do this," she said, holding up the altered metal.

The Willows stared in hushed quiet, aware that as much as Byte didn't understand their ways, they didn't understand his.

"Look!" Peotry called out in sudden delight, pointing at her computer screen. "He does understand, he does!"

And so did they, for nestled comfortably in the heart of a gently shimmering daffodil, waving wildly, was a tiny, bright-eyed Byte.

01010100 01101000 01100101

01000101 01101110 01100100

For similar ages, you might also like:

Piccadilly Mitzie

Dinosaur Boy

Star Games

The Last Garden

For slightly older readers:

The Fantastic Galactic Construction Kit

The Fantastic Prismatic Construction Kit

The Fantastic Chromatic Construction Kit (2013)

The Secret

And for even older readers:

Train Ghost

Miracle Girl

Cool World

Look out for our next book in September 2012

A Boy Arrives *by Stephen Meek*

For more information and a pleasant ten minutes, visit:

www.hawkwoodbooks.co.uk

Lightning Source UK Ltd.
Milton Keynes UK
UKOW030735140312

188942UK00003B/5/P